Terri waited an  sidelines.

"Listen, we hav............ she said to him as he strolled up to her, unstrapping his helmet.

He looked upset. "I don't really feel like talking right now, Terri. Can't it wait till after tomorrow?"

From the look on his face Terri knew she'd been right. Something had gone wrong with his vision. "I can't let you go out on the field tomorrow if there's something wrong with your eyes!" she blurted out.

Ken glared at her. "Quit mothering me, Terri. That stuff was fine back when I needed it, but I can see just fine now. I don't need you playing nurse."

Terri stared at him, completely stunned. "I'm just trying to—"

"Trying to keep me from doing what I love," Ken finished bitterly. "You ought to be a little less protective, Terri. Take a lesson from Claire. Her motto is, 'I'd rather die than quit.' "

"Quit telling me how great Claire is," Terri retorted, glaring back at him. "I'm sick and tired of hearing it. Claire wasn't there when you thought you couldn't even make it down the hallway without help!"

Ken backed up, his blue eyes filled with anger. "If you think a good relationship is based on gratitude, Terri, then you're crazy!"

Bantam Books in the Sweet Valley High Series
Ask your bookseller for the books you have missed

#1 DOUBLE LOVE
#2 SECRETS
#3 PLAYING WITH FIRE
#4 POWER PLAY
#5 ALL NIGHT LONG
#6 DANGEROUS LOVE
#7 DEAR SISTER
#8 HEARTBREAKER
#9 RACING HEARTS
#10 WRONG KIND OF GIRL
#11 TOO GOOD TO BE TRUE
#12 WHEN LOVE DIES
#13 KIDNAPPED!
#14 DECEPTIONS
#15 PROMISES
#16 RAGS TO RICHES
#17 LOVE LETTERS
#18 HEAD OVER HEELS
#19 SHOWDOWN
#20 CRASH LANDING!
#21 RUNAWAY
#22 TOO MUCH IN LOVE
#23 SAY GOODBYE
#24 MEMORIES
#25 NOWHERE TO RUN
#26 HOSTAGE!
#27 LOVESTRUCK
#28 ALONE IN THE CROWD
#29 BITTER RIVALS
#30 JEALOUS LIES
#31 TAKING SIDES
#32 THE NEW JESSICA
#33 STARTING OVER
#34 FORBIDDEN LOVE
#35 OUT OF CONTROL
#36 LAST CHANCE

#37 RUMORS
#38 LEAVING HOME
#39 SECRET ADMIRER
#40 ON THE EDGE
#41 OUTCAST
#42 CAUGHT IN THE MIDDLE
#43 HARD CHOICES
#44 PRETENSES
#45 FAMILY SECRETS
#46 DECISIONS
#47 TROUBLEMAKER
#48 SLAM BOOK FEVER
#49 PLAYING FOR KEEPS
#50 OUT OF REACH
#51 AGAINST THE ODDS
#52 WHITE LIES
#53 SECOND CHANCE
#54 TWO-BOY WEEKEND
#55 PERFECT SHOT
#56 LOST AT SEA
#57 TEACHER CRUSH
#58 BROKENHEARTED
#59 IN LOVE AGAIN
#60 THAT FATAL NIGHT
#61 BOY TROUBLE
#62 WHO'S WHO?
#63 THE NEW ELIZABETH
#64 THE GHOST OF
     TRICIA MARTIN
#65 TROUBLE AT HOME
#66 WHO'S TO BLAME?
#67 THE PARENT PLOT
#68 THE LOVE BET
#69 FRIEND AGAINST FRIEND
#70 MS. QUARTERBACK

Super Editions: PERFECT SUMMER
                SPECIAL CHRISTMAS
                SPRING BREAK
                MALIBU SUMMER
                WINTER CARNIVAL
                SPRING FEVER

Super Thrillers: DOUBLE JEOPARDY
                 ON THE RUN
                 NO PLACE TO HIDE
                 DEADLY SUMMER

Super Stars: LILA'S STORY
                BRUCE'S STORY

SWEET VALLEY HIGH

Ms. Quarterback

Written by
Kate William

Created by
FRANCINE PASCAL

BANTAM BOOKS
NEW YORK · TORONTO · LONDON · SYDNEY · AUCKLAND

RL 6, age 12 and up

MS. QUARTERBACK
A Bantam Book / November 1990

Sweet Valley High is a registered trademark of Francine Pascal

Conceived by Francine Pascal

Produced by Daniel Weiss Associates, Inc.
33 West 17th Street
New York, NY 10011

Cover art by James Mathewuse

All rights reserved.
Copyright © 1990 by Francine Pascal.
Cover art copyright © 1990 by Daniel Weiss Associates, Inc.
No part of this book may be reproduced or transmitted
in any form or by any means, electronic or mechanical,
including photocopying, recording, or by any information
storage and retrieval system, without permission in
writing from the publisher.
For information address: Bantam Books.

ISBN 0-553-28767-2

Published simultaneously in the United States and Canada

Bantam Books are published by Bantam Books, a division of Bantam Doubleday
Dell Publishing Group, Inc. Its trademark, consisting of the words "Bantam
Books" and the portrayal of a rooster, is Registered in U.S. Patent and Trademark
Office and in other countries. Marca Registrada. Bantam Books, 666 Fifth Avenue,
New York, New York 10103.

PRINTED IN THE UNITED STATES OF AMERICA

OPM   0 9 8 7 6 5 4 3 2 1

Ms. Quarterback

One

"Hey, Liz! Aren't you going to the pep rally?" Enid Rollins called out as the two girls crossed paths in the crowded hallway of Sweet Valley High.

Elizabeth Wakefield gave her best friend a quick wave. "I've got to meet Todd at my locker first. Go on, Enid. We'll meet you in the gym!"

Elizabeth ran a hand through her long blond hair and strained her eyes for a glimpse of Todd Wilkins, her boyfriend. The corridor was packed with students heading in the opposite direction, toward the gymnasium, and Elizabeth felt a little bit like a salmon swimming upstream.

The pep rally had been organized by Coach Schultz to support the Gladiators, Sweet Valley High's football team, before their game that weekend against the Palisades Pumas. The Pumas

1

were one of Sweet Valley High's biggest rivals, and the next day's game was the last in the season before the all-important match with Big Mesa two weeks later. Big Mesa was the only team with more wins that season than Sweet Valley. If Sweet Valley could beat them, the Gladiators would have a chance to go to the state play-offs.

Elizabeth was really looking forward to the pep rally. Sweet Valley High had been through some rough turmoil in the past few weeks, and like a number of other students, Elizabeth was hoping the rally would help revive school spirit.

She caught sight of Todd up ahead. He was leaning back against her locker, tapping one foot impatiently.

"Hey," he said, giving her a kiss on the cheek when she came up to him. "I was getting worried about you. Is this the same Elizabeth who's always three minutes early?" he added teasingly.

Elizabeth laughed. She was used to friendly jibes about her punctuality. Unlike her twin sister, Jessica, who never even wore a watch, Elizabeth could always be counted on to be on time.

"I was talking to John Pfeifer about doing some new sports pieces for the newspaper. I guess we lost track of time." She spun her locker combination, opened her locker, and stuffed her books inside. "So, what do you think is going to happen at this rally? Do you

2

think Coach Schultz is going to spring the news about Scott?"

Elizabeth had heard that Scott Trost, the team's first-string quarterback, was failing history and Spanish classes. If the rumor was true, Scott would probably go on academic probation. He would be suspended from the team until his grades went up.

"Hey, you know that's inside information," Todd said, his brown eyes sparkling mischievously. "You newspaper reporters always know the truth before anyone else."

Todd was right. Almost no one knew about Scott yet. Elizabeth had heard the rumor from John Pfeifer, sports editor of *The Oracle*, but she'd been sworn to secrecy.

"News reporters may know," she teased him, ruffling his curly brown hair, "but so do their boyfriends!"

Todd put his arm around her, and Elizabeth felt a surge of warmth run through her. Even though she and Todd had been steady boyfriend and girlfriend for a long time, she still felt a thrill when he hugged her.

"Besides," Elizabeth went on as she and Todd walked to the rally, "I don't think the rumor about Scott can be kept quiet for long—not with so much riding on the Gladiators' performance in the next couple of weeks." She thought for a moment, then added, "Maybe today's the day

3

we'll learn more about that girl who wants to be quarterback."

Elizabeth had recently run a questionnaire in the school paper asking students what they would most like to see changed at Sweet Valley High.

Some of the suggestions she received had really surprised her. In fact, some had been extremely troubling, dealing with issues of discrimination. One girl, who had responded anonymously, had written that she didn't see why a girl shouldn't try out for a boys' team, even for quarterback of the varsity football team.

Elizabeth wasn't completely sure that Scott Trost would be suspended as quarterback. But if he was, maybe whoever wrote that complaint would be bold enough to actually try out for the position.

Todd rolled his eyes. "Liz, that was just a joke. No girl in her right mind would try out for quarterback."

Elizabeth shook her head. "I think you're wrong," she told him. "I'm pretty sure she was serious, and I think it's great!"

"Listen, I'm all for a girl quarterback," Todd said, giving Elizabeth's shoulder an affectionate squeeze. "But I think I may be an exception, if the other guys on the basketball team are any indication. A lot of them are pretty chauvinistic, and I bet the football team is the same way."

Elizabeth shrugged. "Well, maybe whoever it is will have the chance to prove to them that they're wrong!"

When they got to the gymnasium, Elizabeth scanned the crowded bleachers, trying to locate Enid.

"Liz! Todd! Over here!"

Elizabeth heard Enid's voice calling out to them, and she looked up to see her friend sitting high up.

Elizabeth waved back and called, "We're coming!" It took them a while to negotiate their way up the bleachers. First Winston Egbert, the clown of the junior class, pretended he was going to trip Todd, then gave him a high-five. "Very funny, Egbert," Todd muttered. Before they got a step farther, Aaron Dallas stopped Todd to ask him something. And several other friends called out to them before they at last sat down next to Enid, feigning exhaustion.

"Sorry. We got intercepted," Todd joked.

Enid's green eyes were shining. "Where have you two been? I've been going nuts up here. Have you heard the news?"

"What news?" Elizabeth asked, looking out over the gym as she shrugged out of her cardigan sweater. The football team was lining up on one side of the gym, and across from them

5

the cheerleaders, including Elizabeth's twin sister, Jessica, were forming one of their famous pyramids.

"Scott Trost," Enid whispered excitedly. "He flunked another history test this week. Coach Schultz has been talking to Chrome Dome all day, but it doesn't look like there's any way around it." "Chrome Dome" was the students' nickname for their bald principal, Mr. Cooper. "Scott's on probation for the rest of the term—meaning, the rest of the football season!"

Elizabeth and Todd stared at each other, then at Enid. "Wow," Elizabeth said. "I guess it's really true." So much for the rumor. Scott's suspension was finally out in the open.

"Poor Scott," Todd commented. "He must be going out of his mind. He's had such a great season so far."

"I know. Especially coming in the way he did after Ken's accident . . ." Enid said slowly.

Up until a few months ago Ken Matthews had been the Gladiators' captain and quarterback. Elizabeth had heard that he was actually pro material and was being approached by some scouts. At any rate, there was no doubt that he would have gotten a football scholarship at a good school. On top of being talented, he was handsome and friendly. It seemed that he had everything going for him, his whole future wrapped up—until the terrible night when a drunk driver skidded out of control on a deserted, rainy road, forcing Ken's car off the road and head-on into a tree.

Elizabeth's head turned automatically in Ken Matthews's direction. *Looking at him now, you'd never know what he's been through*, Elizabeth thought. He was every bit as good-looking and strong as he had ever been. Sitting next to his girlfriend, Terri Adams, he looked cheerful and relaxed.

But for a while it had seemed as though Ken's entire future had been knocked off the road along with his car. Elizabeth clearly remembered hearing the shocking news that a head injury had caused swelling that had left Ken blind. He had to forget foorball and a future in the pros! For Ken, just getting down the hallway had turned into a major feat. He had worked really hard to get back on his feet and adjust, both on his own and with the help of his physical therapist, Ron Jablonski. And Terri had been there to support him every step of the way, too.

"I wonder if Ken's heard the news about Scott yet," Enid said, following Elizabeth's gaze. "Now that he can see again, do you think . . ." Her voice trailed off, but Elizabeth knew what her friend was thinking.

"Ken wouldn't be ready for that kind of competition right now," Elizabeth said, shaking her head. "Besides, his vision still isn't back one hundred percent. Terri told me it could be months before it is."

Todd frowned. "I don't know about that. I played basketball with Ken last Saturday. If that guy can't see, then he's got some kind of guardian angel telling him where the basket is," he said enthusiastically. "I think you're onto something, Enid. If I know Ken Matthews, there's no way he's going to sit back and let an opportunity like this pass by. If Scott is out, somebody's going to have to take over the ballgame. And Ken's the obvious choice."

Elizabeth didn't answer. She didn't want to sound defeatist, but Ken hadn't been out on the field for a long time. Would he really be in any shape to take over as quarterback?

Jessica Wakefield jumped down out of the pyramid formation and looked critically at the other cheerleaders, a frown on her face. Couldn't they see that the cheers were getting old? Jessica fumed. It seemed to her that some people had actually stopped paying attention to the cheerleaders—and that was something Jessica wouldn't stand for.

Except for her red-and-white cheerleading uniform, Jessica looked so much like her twin sister, Elizabeth, it would have been impossible for a stranger to tell them apart. Each was blond, slim, and graced with quintessential California beauty. Each had sparkling blue-green eyes and a tiny dimple in her left cheek that showed when she smiled. And each wore a gold lavaliere necklace, a birthday present from their parents on their sixteenth birthday.

But apart from their identical appearance, they couldn't be more different. Elizabeth was the "responsible" twin—that was the way Jessica always put it. She was serious and liked to take things slowly and steadily, whereas Jessica was impulsive and liked change and excitement. Elizabeth hoped to become a writer one day, and she dedicated long hours to her work on the school paper, *The Oracle*. When she took on a cause, she did it wholeheartedly and saw it through to the end. Unlike Elizabeth, Jessica's interests were constantly changing. She had a different hobby and a different boyfriend practically every day of the week. When life got too dull for her, Jessica wouldn't hesitate to liven things up, even at the expense of her twin.

Jessica pulled impatiently at her uniform, although it fit perfectly. Ordinarily there was nothing she loved more than a pep rally. It was fun getting to wear her uniform to school, and even better doing cheers in front of the entire student body. She knew she looked good in her red-and-white pleated skirt and white knit sweater, and she always enjoyed being the center of attention.

"I can't stand that rah-rah-rah one," she complained to Robin Wilson, who, with Jessica, was cocaptain of the cheerleaders. "Can't we do any better? They must have heard this cheer seven billion times."

Robin looked at Jessica questioningly. "And it always gets the crowd going. I don't see what's the matter with it."

Jessica tossed back her blond hair and surveyed the group of cheerleaders, eight in all, counting Robin and herself. "I just think this cheering squad needs a little new blood in it."

"We've already had tryouts, Jess," Robin reminded her.

Amy Sutton, another cheerleader and one of Jessica's closest friends, danced over. "What are you two arguing about? By the way, do we have to do the pyramid again? I'm getting a little sick of it."

"See?" Jessica said triumphantly. "Amy's the newest member of the squad, and even *she* thinks the cheers are getting tired."

Robin opened her mouth to say something but was interrupted when Maria Santelli came rushing over from the bleachers. "You guys, did you hear the news about Scott? He's off the team for the rest of the season!"

Amy Sutton's gray eyes widened. She had started dating Scott when he took over as first-string quarterback after Ken's accident. She had really been looking forward to basking in Scott's glory during the weeks ahead. "He hasn't been quarterback that long. How can he possibly be off the team already?" she demanded.

"Academic probation," Maria explained. "He's failing history."

"That's ridiculous," Amy muttered. Scowling, she bent over and pretended to retie her shoelace.

Jessica couldn't resist a little dig. "Maybe Ken will try out for the spot again. That would be kind of awkward for you, wouldn't it?" she teased.

Two spots of color flared in Amy's cheeks. The fact that she had coldheartedly dropped Ken after his accident and then kindled a romance with his replacement was not something she liked to be reminded of.

"I'm going to get a drink of water," she snapped and stormed off across the gym.

By now the entire gymnasium was buzzing with the news of Scott's probation, and when Coach Schultz stepped up to the microphone, it was hard to hear his voice. "Please!" he cried, putting up his hand to silence everyone. "I do not want rumors of any kind marring our team's performance," he said calmly. "Our football team is one of the strongest in the state." Loud cheer-

11

ing broke out, and the coach had to wait for it to die down before continuing. "We're going to go into tomorrow's game against the Palisades Pumas with our current lineup. But after tomorrow, due to some reorganization—"

This phrase met with an intense reaction from the audience. A loud hum of voices spread through the bleachers, and the coach had to speak loudly to be heard over the noise.

"—we will be holding tryouts, on Monday after school in the playing field, for the position of quarterback."

Jessica's eyes flew up to the spot in the bleachers where Ken Matthews was sitting next to Terri. It was clear from the expression on his face that the news about Scott had taken Ken by surprise. But would Ken take advantage of his friend's suspension to get back on the team? And, Jessica wondered, what would happen if he tried out and failed!

When the rally ended, Terri Adams took a deep breath and pushed her way through the crowd to the corner of the gymnasium where the football players were standing. As the new assistant manager for the Gladiators—she had recently been promoted from assistant statistician—she could have stood with them during the pep rally. But since Ken had left the team, she tended

12

to minimize her role at public events like this one. She preferred to sit up in the stands and keep him company.

Terri was surprised by the coach's announcement. She had been hearing rumors about Scott for a while now, but she hadn't expected him to be suspended *now*, before the big game against Big Mesa. It was common knowledge on the bench that Scott had overextended himself this semester. Playing football was one thing, but taking over the starring position and trying to juggle college prep classes at the same time was something else. Not to mention that the second-string quarterback had injured his hamstring, which meant that Scott had no backup. Scott was disciplined and hardworking, but he wasn't as gifted an athlete as Ken. Terri knew he had felt that he needed to add to his practice time in an attempt to improve himself. He'd let football take over his entire life. Now he was out, and the team had lost its most important player.

Terri knew the news had shocked Ken, too. He had looked completely flabbergasted at first, but then he seemed to tense with excitement. With all the noise of the pep rally, they hadn't been able to talk about it, but Terri was sure Ken was considering trying out, and that worried her a little.

"Hey, Terri!" John Pfeifer hurried over to her.

13

"What's Ken saying about the coach's news? You think there's any chance he'll feel up to trying out for his old spot on the team?"

Within seconds the petite, pretty junior was surrounded. Terri had known most of the guys on the team for years now. Usually she felt as at ease with them as she did with her own brothers. But suddenly she felt nervous. Everyone crowded around asking for information about Ken. Zack Johnson, a sophomore linebacker and one of her closest friends, rushed up to ask about Ken, too. They all wanted to know the same thing: What was Ken planning to do now? Was he going to try out for his old position, or let someone else take the place?

"I don't know," Terri said, forcing a smile. "You'll have to ask Ken what he plans to do."

It *was* exciting to think about Ken playing again, but was he ready for all this pressure to perform? He'd been doing incredibly well—better than his doctors had hoped. But, after all, he *had* suffered a serious head injury. Terri wanted Ken to be happy, but she also knew he was still having some trouble with his eyes—not a lot, but enough for her to worry about him.

Clearly the whole school wanted Ken back as quarterback. She just hoped Ken still felt that *he* was the one who would make the choice.

"I'm psyched!" Zack exclaimed. "I just know Ken's going to be back on the team!"

"It's going to be like old times," added Danny Porter, Sweet Valley's wide receiver. "I'm sorry about Scott, but this is the perfect chance for Ken. He's the only one who can help us wipe out Big Mesa!"

Terri bit her lip. Everyone was already assuming Ken would try out. "We can't decide Ken's plans for him. He'll have to make his own decision," she said.

Terri could tell by the surprised looks Zack and John gave her that her words had come out a little more negatively than she'd intended. If he wanted to try out for quarterback again, she would be behind him all the way. But she didn't want to see him pressured into it. Not by the coach, and not by the other guys on the team.

Two

"Wow, that was some pep rally," Elizabeth said as she and Enid made their way down the bleachers. Todd had stayed behind to talk to Aaron Dallas. "What do you think is going to happen? Do you think Ken's really ready to try out for quarterback again?"

"I hope so," Enid said. "I want Sweet Valley High to really win big against Big Mesa."

Elizabeth's eyebrows shot up. "Even with Hugh cheering for the other side?" she teased. Hugh Grayson, Enid's boyfriend, was a senior at Big Mesa.

Enid frowned. "Lately it seems as though we're more on opposite teams than ever," she said quietly.

Elizabeth gave her friend a concerned look. The last she'd heard, things between Enid and

16

Hugh were great. But from Enid's comment, that wasn't true anymore. "Why?" she asked. "Is anything wrong?"

"No," Enid said. "It's just . . ." Her voice trailed off, and Elizabeth could tell from her expression that this wasn't the time or the place to talk about it. "I'll tell you more later," Enid promised. "But let's just put it this way: My loyalties are definitely with Sweet Valley High these days!"

Enid said goodbye, and Elizabeth watched her thoughtfully as she hurried out of the gym. Elizabeth knew Enid was really serious about Hugh. She hated to think the couple was going through a rough time.

"All right, Liz Wakefield, get your head out of the clouds."

Elizabeth turned and smiled as Todd came up from behind.

"I'm worried about Enid," she told him. She filled Todd in on what had just happened, finishing with, "And I thought they were getting *more* serious about each other!"

"Maybe they just had a fight," Todd said. "You know how these things go. They'll probably make up this weekend, and everything will be fine again."

Elizabeth wasn't so sure. If it was Jessica they were talking about, maybe. But Enid didn't say things rashly. If she had doubts about Hugh, she probably had a good reason.

Looking into Todd's chocolate-brown eyes, Elizabeth couldn't help thinking back to the hard times they had gone through in their relationship. When Todd's family was transferred to the East Coast, they had decided to split up rather than carry on a long-distance romance. She felt like the luckiest girl in the world when she was given a second chance with Todd after his family had moved back to Sweet Valley. They both had had other relationships while they were separated, but since Todd's return the bond between them had been stronger than ever. Still, Elizabeth remembered how agonizing the whole situation had been, and she could sympathize with Enid.

Elizabeth's thoughts were interrupted when Penny Ayala called to her from the other side of the gymnasium. A tall, lanky senior with light brown hair and a warm smile, Penny was the editor in chief of the student newspaper. The minute she saw Penny, Elizabeth remembered that she was supposed to have organized an interview that week with Claire Middleton, a transfer student from Palisades High.

This wasn't the first time lately that she had been absentminded about an assignment for *The Oracle*, and it troubled her. "I can't believe I forgot to talk to Claire," Elizabeth said to Todd.

"I'd better go talk to Penny right now." She gave Todd a quick goodbye kiss and hurried over to Penny, who was looking through some papers on her clipboard. "Penny, I haven't forgotten about interviewing Claire. I just didn't have time between classes to talk to you about it," Elizabeth began.

Penny put up a hand to stop her. "Don't worry, Liz. It's fine. I just wanted to let you know that Claire is about as hard to pin down as you are, so I took the liberty of setting up an interview slot with her. Since classes are over for the day, I thought you two could meet right now."

"That sounds fine," Elizabeth said.

"Great," Penny told her. "I'd like to see your draft as soon as possible, so we can get the story out in next week's paper. And remember, we're running this along with some stories on other students who have transferred to Sweet Valley High in the past year."

Elizabeth nodded and took out the little notepad she carried around in her pocketbook. "Any special angle you're hoping for?"

Penny shrugged. "Just the stuff we talked about at our last meeting: differences between Sweet Valley High and her old school; her feelings about being a transfer student. Just use your ace reporting skills!"

Elizabeth laughed. "I'll find Claire right away,"

she promised. "And I'll have a draft of the story to you on Monday."

"Good," Penny said. "Oh—I almost forgot," she added. "John just told me he's going to need some extra help with the sports supplement he's putting together. He wants a lot of extra coverage on this new quarterback spot. So when you finish with Claire's interview, maybe you could help him out."

"Sure!" Elizabeth said enthusiastically. She was always happy to put in extra work on the paper, but she had a special reason for wanting to cover the tryouts. If there was a girl who wanted to try out for quarterback, Elizabeth was dying to meet her!

Twenty minutes later Elizabeth was sitting on one of the bleached maple benches in the courtyard of the high school, her pad and a pen in her lap. The courtyard was a favorite place for students to spend quiet time during lunch hours. Ceramic pots of flowers brightened the terrace, and the benches were tucked in among trees and bushes, allowing a bit of privacy.

Claire Middleton was right on time for the interview. Elizabeth wasn't sure what to expect. She had spoken to Claire once or twice before, but Claire was very shy and always seemed to run off before they could get to know each other. As Claire came over, Elizabeth smiled, hoping to put her more at ease.

Claire had a slightly tomboyish appearance, but it was softened by the waves of long, pretty dark hair that fell around her face. Her oval face was warmed by a beautiful smile and a spattering of freckles across her cheeks and nose, and her eyes were an unusual pale green shade. In fact, the tomboyish look came more from her clothes than her face or figure. This afternoon, for instance, Claire's slim figure was hidden by a loose-fitting red cotton sweater and a pair of worn jeans.

"Hi," Elizabeth greeted her as Claire sat down next to her on the bench. "I guess Penny explained that we're putting together a story on new students and that we wanted to do a special interview with you?"

Claire reddened and looked down. "That's what she said. But I don't think I have enough to tell you to make a whole story."

Elizabeth laughed. "Just relax. By the time I've finished firing questions at you, you'll probably think I'm trying to write a whole novel."

Claire smiled uneasily but didn't say anything.

"So," Elizabeth began, "your family just moved, right? And that's why you left Palisades High?"

Claire nodded. "Yes. We bought a new house, and that put me into a different school district."

21

Elizabeth wrote that down. "Any particular reason for the move?"

"We thought—" Claire broke off, and Elizabeth sensed she seemed even more uncomfortable. "No, not really," Claire said abruptly. "My parents wanted to move to a smaller house." She looked down at her hands.

Elizabeth looked at Claire, not sure what to ask next. Her question had been pretty standard, yet the way Claire answered made Elizabeth feel that she had been prying and rude. "Well, let's see," Elizabeth said after clearing her throat. "What are your impressions of Sweet Valley High so far? Do you see any special difference between this place and your old school?"

Claire hesitated before answering. "The kids here seem nice and friendly. But I've been pretty busy studying. I haven't met very many people yet."

Elizabeth smiled sympathetically. "It's got to be hard, switching schools in the middle of the year. I'm sure you'll meet a lot of people soon."

Claire nodded but continued to look down into her lap rather than meet Elizabeth's gaze. Claire obviously didn't like to be in the spotlight, but it seemed to Elizabeth that her reaction was extreme. There had to be some way to get Claire to loosen up, she thought.

Elizabeth made a few more notes, then asked

casually, "Do you have any special hobbies? Any clubs you might join?"

Claire's pale green eyes lit up, and she leaned forward on the bench. "I like football a lot," she said eagerly.

"Football?" Elizabeth took in the animated expression on Claire's face. Was it possible *Claire* was the girl who had sent in the survey response about wanting to try out for the boys' team? Elizabeth decided to pursue the topic. "Did you go to the pep rally? It must be strange for you, attending a rally for a game that will be against your old school."

Claire nodded and said, "It's a little weird, but football's a great game no matter where it's played. Besides, the Gladiators are really good." After a minute's pause, she added, "Oh, and I like other sports, too. Running, cycling. I guess you could say I'm a little bit of a fitness fanatic."

Elizabeth smiled. Talking about football had definitely sparked Claire's interest. In ten seconds she had gone from being withdrawn and shy to being totally involved in the interview.

Scribbling down the information, Elizabeth pressed, "Any particular reason you're such a football buff? That's not so typical for girls."

"I've always liked it," Claire said, pushing her dark hair back and giving a small shrug. "And I'm pretty intense about the things I like. I'm not good at doing things halfway."

23

"Great!" Elizabeth said, writing quickly. It was looking more and more as if Claire were the mystery girl football player! She looked over her notes. "Is there anything else? Any brothers or sisters who have transferred to Sweet Valley High, too?"

Claire's bright expression was suddenly replaced by a frown, and she slumped over her books. "No. No brothers or sisters," she said. Looking nervously at Elizabeth, she gathered her books and stood up. "Sorry," she added. "I told you, I'm not exactly a thrill to interview."

Elizabeth put the top back on her pen. "You've been great, Claire. Thanks for letting me take up your time," she said with a smile, even though in truth she was a little disappointed by the sudden change in Claire. And just when she was really starting to let go and talk about herself.

Claire rushed off toward the parking lot, leaving Elizabeth to stare after her. It was strange, Elizabeth thought. Claire could be open one minute and aloof the next. And the way she practically ran away just when the interview was getting interesting made it seem as if she had something to hide.

But Claire had no reason to hide anything, Elizabeth reminded herself. If the interview hadn't gone well, it was her own fault, not Claire's. Maybe she had somehow insulted

Claire. She went over all the questions she had asked, but they seemed pretty ordinary and inoffensive. Elizabeth hoped she would get another chance to talk to Claire, or else she wouldn't have much of a story to write up for Penny.

"Hi. Anyone home?" Elizabeth called, opening the front door of the split-level home the Wakefields owned on a tree-lined side street in Sweet Valley.

She heard a chair scrape in the kitchen. "I'm in here, Liz! But I'm on the phone," Jessica called back.

Elizabeth laughed. Jessica was always on the phone. She crouched down to scratch Prince Albert, the Wakefields' golden Labrador.

A few minutes later Jessica bounded into the living room, still in her cheerleading uniform. "So, what did you think of the pep rally today?" Jessica asked. "The coach's news about Scott was a real bombshell, wasn't it?"

"I'd heard some rumors about it before, so I guess I wasn't really shocked," said Elizabeth. "But it changed the tone of the rally, that's for sure."

Jessica nodded. "It's kind of hard to concentrate on school spirit when no one even knows who's going to be leading the team."

"I know," Elizabeth said slowly, disappointment showing on her face. "Given what's happened at school over the past couple of weeks, I was hoping this pep rally would, you know, kind of bring us all back together."

"I know what you mean," Jessica agreed.

A shocking incident had recently upset the entire school. Andy Jenkins, a junior who had just won a prominent local science scholarship, had been brutally attacked by a group of guys, just because he was black. Charlie Cashman, a well-known troublemaker at Sweet Valley High, had been the ringleader of the terrible attack, but Neil Freemount, a friend of Elizabeth's, had also been involved. The incident had stirred up painful feelings in the whole community. Everyone was still talking about it, and several students and teachers, including Elizabeth and Jessica, were working on a racial awareness program for Sweet Valley High.

"It worries me how many people are ignoring what happened to Andy," Elizabeth said. "I think a lot of kids feel that pretending it never happened is the only way to make it go away."

Jessica shrugged. As usual, her attention was beginning to drift. "It's hard getting people to agree to do anything different," she said vaguely, looking down at her cheerleading outfit with a frown. Then her blue-green eyes brightened. "But who knows. Maybe if Ken tries out for quarterback again . . . well, then we might at least get back some of our old school spirit."

"Maybe you're right," Elizabeth agreed half-heartedly.

Elizabeth watched distractedly while Jessica began to leaf through a fashion magazine on the coffee table. "Hey," she said suddenly. "Speaking of new things and new people, what's your impression of Claire Middleton? Do you like her?"

"I don't really know her," Jessica replied. "But Amy and I have been talking about trying to get her to join the sorority. She looks like a Pi Beta Alpha."

Elizabeth was surprised. "Really?" Jessica was president of the exclusive sorority, which tended to attract girls like Amy Sutton and Lila Fowler, who weren't exactly two of Elizabeth's favorite people. Amy was absolutely boy-crazy, and Lila, the daughter of one of the richest men in Sweet Valley, was as self-centered and spoiled as anyone Elizabeth had ever met.

She couldn't see Claire fitting in with that crowd, and frankly, she was surprised that Jessica could.

But then, why not? Elizabeth reasoned. Pi Beta Alpha had come under fire lately for being too "exclusive." Several people had complained about that in *The Oracle*'s recent survey, the same survey in which the comment about girls

27

playing football had been made. And Elizabeth had to agree with them. Even though she was a member of the sorority, she rarely attended meetings. The members of Pi Beta Alpha seemed more concerned with their social status than with the good of Sweet Valley High. If Jessica was trying to change Pi Beta Alpha's exclusive approach and be friendly to Claire, Elizabeth supposed she ought to be glad.

Even so, she didn't think Claire was the sorority type. She wasn't at all social, from what Elizabeth had seen. But maybe Jessica would be able to get further with Claire Middleton than she herself had!

Three

Terri woke up early Saturday morning feeling tired and out of sorts. She hadn't slept very well the night before, and even a brisk shower failed to lift her spirits. As she brushed her shoulder-length light brown hair, she checked her reflection in the mirror over her dresser and saw that there were circles under her eyes.

And her little brother's remarks at the breakfast table only made her feel worse.

"Hey," Mark mumbled through a mouthful of cereal. "Looks like Sweet Valley's going to get smeared. What are you guys going to do, Terri? How are you going to find yourselves a new quarterback before the Big Mesa game?"

Usually Terri was able to handle Mark's endless questions about the team with a good sense of humor. But that morning she really didn't want to think about football.

"I'm sure Coach Schultz will think of something," she said flatly, reaching across the table for the cereal. She didn't bother to tell him about the tryouts, but apparently he already knew.

"Why doesn't Ken try out?" Mark continued in the same blunt tone. "His eyes are better, aren't they?"

Terri poured herself some cereal. Ken was part of the reason she was in a bad mood to begin with. "Why don't you mind your own business, Mark?" she snapped.

She was surprised at how angrily the words came out. She almost never got cross with her little brother, not even when he pulled his usual twelve-year-old antics.

"Sor-*ry*," Mark said, whistling. "Excuse me for living!"

Terri picked up the newspaper, trying to ignore how confused and frustrated she felt. But without thinking she had picked up the sports page. Terri groaned. She couldn't seem to escape being reminded of Ken, one way or another.

Ordinarily Terri loved to think about Ken. She loved talking about him and even just saying his name. But the night before they'd gone out and had a terrible time, and she was still upset about it.

30

The evening had started out perfectly, just like all their dates, with Ken meeting her at her house. They had planned to go to the movies with John Pfeifer and his girlfriend, Jennifer Mitchell, but nothing had worked out right. First of all, John had been late picking them up, so they had ended up missing the movie. Then Jennifer had suggested stopping off at the Dairi Burger, "just to see who's around." Terri had thought it would be fun, but no sooner had they walked into the place than things had begun to fall apart—at least as far as Terri was concerned.

Ken had immediately been surrounded by kids who wanted to know what he was going to do, if he was ready to try out, how his eyes were. At first it had been great seeing how Ken had loved the attention. It obviously meant a lot to him that the other students were behind him and wanted him back on the team.

But after a few minutes, Terri had started to feel left out. No one said very much to her, and worst of all, *Ken* had ignored her, too. After ten minutes or so, she had gone over to the booth where John and Jennifer were sitting, and the three of them ordered something to eat. But Ken had stood around talking with his "fans" until the food came. And even then he hadn't really joined in their conversation.

Terri hadn't meant to, but she started to sulk. For the first time she realized that if

Ken decided to try out for quarterback, it would mean a big change in their relationship. He would be more caught up in the game and would have less time for her. The more she thought about it, the more upset she'd become. She wished she could be happier for Ken, but she couldn't help the way she felt.

Terri hadn't been her usual self for the rest of the evening, and eventually Ken noticed how quiet she was. When he asked her about it, she tried to make up an excuse, but she knew it sounded pretty lame.

"Well, now that I may be getting back on the football team, I hope you're not going to turn out to be the kind of girl who gets jealous whenever you spend time away from her—at practice or talking about the game or whatever." He shrugged. "You know, the kind of girl who acts like you're a jerk just because you're not hanging all over her every minute."

Terri just stared at him. She was hardly that kind of girl! She loved football. And how could he say that in front of John and Jennifer—she was so embarrassed!

Still, in the back of her mind Terri knew that what Ken had said was partly true. She *had* been upset because he'd been ignoring her.

When he dropped her off later, she'd kissed him good night as if everything were just fine. She hadn't wanted to let him accuse her of being clingy or demanding. If he wanted to spend the evening talking to everyone but her, that was fine with her!

But she didn't feel fine this morning. In fact, she felt awful.

"Hey," Mark said in an annoyed voice, causing Terri to look up. "I asked you twice already, Terri. Are you going to read the sports page, or can I?"

"Here," Terri muttered, pushing it across the table to him.

She tried to shake off her unhappiness. It had just been an off night for them both, she told herself. She had absolutely no reason to feel so uneasy. She knew Ken still loved her. In fact, he was expecting her any minute. She was picking him up at his house, and they were going to school together to watch the Gladiators play the Pumas. Today would be Scott's last game as quarterback. It was sure to be exciting and lots of fun.

So why did she still feel something was very wrong?

As she drove over to Ken's house in her mother's Volvo, Terri's mind wandered back over the months she and Ken had been together.

She had to admit, the way she and Ken had gotten together was pretty unusual. Long before his accident, Terri had had a big crush on Ken. Whenever she had seen him she'd gotten sweaty hands and a dry throat, her heart had thumped madly, and she had felt completely tongue-tied. And she had seen him often, because at that time she had been the team's assistant statistician. She'd also seen enough to know that she wasn't the only girl at school who was interested—very interested—in Ken.

It had really hurt Terri to watch girls like Amy Sutton throw themselves at Ken. She knew she liked Ken for his *real* self—not just because he was the Gladiators' football hero. Sure, she had admired him for that, too, but it had been only one of the qualities she liked about him. Yes, he was handsome and had a great build. But more important to her had been Ken's good sense of humor. He was modest, and he cared about his friends. He was loyal, responsible, a great guy. Those were the real reasons Terri cared so much for him.

Before Ken's accident Terri never would have thought she could compete with girls like Amy Sutton. Amy was beautiful, blond, popular, and friends with the "in" crowd—people like Jessica Wakefield and the other girls in Pi Beta Alpha and on the cheerleading squad. Next to Amy, Terri felt drab and tomboyish—totally out of it. It wasn't that Terri thought she was ugly; she knew she was considered pretty by a number of her friends and classmates. But she wasn't in Amy Sutton's league. Everyone knew Amy could wrap whomever she wanted around her little finger.

But then after the accident, things had changed. Few of Ken's friends had known how to cope with the shocking news that he had been seriously hurt. Amy had dropped Ken almost immediately. On top of having to confront the fact that he was blind, maybe for life, Ken had had to face devastating loneliness.

Terri had been afraid to visit Ken in the hospital at first. She had been afraid of saying the wrong thing, or of not knowing what to say at all. But she hadn't been able to stay away; she had cared too much for him. As her visits had become more frequent they both relaxed, and Terri found she was able to be a real friend to Ken. At first she just kept him company, helping him with his homework and keeping him up-to-date on how the Gladiators were doing. Gradually their friendship deepened, but life had gotten complicated when, bit by bit, Ken had become dependent on her.

Terri loved Ken, and while she had wanted him to love her, she hadn't wanted to see him lose his self-reliance; she hadn't wanted their relationship to be based on his need for help. Hard as it was, she had to back off until Ken was ready to regain his independence. And that was when he finally admitted to her that he felt the same way she did. He was in love with her!

They had had wonderful times together. Terri had taken Ken to her favorite places—for long walks on a secluded beach she knew, or to the park. She had been willing to be his "eyes," but he had needed that less and less as his other senses sharpened and he became more confident.

Then, gradually, the miracle had happened. At first Ken could just distinguish shadows and bright light. If she passed her hand in front of his eyes, he could see a faint flicker in his darkness. But each new glimmer of hope had excited Terri as much as Ken. She knew she would never forget the day when he had leaned over and touched her lips with his finger. "Terri," he had said softly, "do you know . . . I can see you? I can see the outline of your face."

Ken had long since left his white cane behind. Now the periods of darkness or blurred vision were the exception, not the rule. *Nothing's changed between us*, Terri reminded herself now, pulling the Volvo into the Matthewses' circular driveway.

But the fact remained that he still did have his bad moments. And Terri was afraid that going back to football too soon might result in some kind of serious relapse.

She shook herself. That was something she could talk about with Ken later on. After all, they shared everything. She loved their talks and couldn't wait to hear all the things he was thinking and feeling about the tryouts.

Looking up, Terri saw that Winston Egbert was standing on the lawn beside Ken's house. "Come on, Matthews! Back up!" he shouted. "I'm coming from center field! I'm flying! I'm letting it go!"

Winston's outburst was followed by a long, high pass across the Matthewses' green lawn. Ken raced backward in a fluid line, his right arm stretched out behind him. Effortless, graceful, he jumped for the ball and made a perfect catch.

"Bravo!" Terri called out, trying to sound more enthusiastic than she felt.

Ken jogged over to her, pushing his hair out of his eyes and giving her that grin of his that made her heart pound. "Hey," he said, tossing the ball from one hand to the other. "What do you think? Winston's been here all morning long, bugging me about trying out for the team again."

Winston huffed up to join them, his face red and sweaty. " 'Course, I thought about trying out myself," he joked to Terri. "But my passing arm's a little off. Besides, I think I should save

37

my athletic prowess for bigger things. The Super Bowl, maybe."

Terri laughed, but the glance she gave Ken was uncertain. "Are you really thinking about trying out?" she asked.

"He's golden. You can't touch him," Winston said quickly. "Why not?"

"I feel good," Ken said, looking straight at Terri. "I'm rusty, of course, but I think I can get back in shape pretty fast."

Terri bit her lip. She knew she should wait until they were alone to talk about it, but the words just seemed to fly out of her mouth. "What about when your vision blurs or you get those blackouts?" she asked.

She wished immediately that she could take back her words. Ken had told almost no one that his vision still gave him trouble. It wasn't something she should have blurted out in front of Winston. What was wrong with her?

Ken reddened, and he stared down at the football, trying to make it spin in his hands.

"Blackouts my foot," Winston said loudly. "This guy's the real thing. Come on, Matthews. Show your girlfriend here what you're made of. That'll convince her not to be such a wet blanket."

Terri felt so ashamed. "Sorry about that," she whispered to Ken as Winston set off across the

38

yard to throw another pass. "I don't know what got into me."

Ken shrugged as if it didn't matter. But he wouldn't meet her gaze, and Terri knew she'd hurt him. She could tell by his embarrassed silence that he wasn't going to admit it to her, either, and that made Terri feel even worse.

She had wanted to talk to him and clear things up, but now he was concentrating on throwing a long pass to Winston, who was already running across the lawn. Terri felt the same as she had the night before. They had never had a serious disagreement until this weekend. Now they couldn't have anything else!

"I am *so* sick of these stupid old cheers!" Jessica said crossly, throwing down her pom-poms and glaring at Robin.

Robin shrugged. "I don't see what's so bad about them, Jess. And you shouldn't keep complaining about them. You're dragging down the morale of the whole squad."

It was Saturday afternoon, and the cheerleaders were practicing out on the playing field behind the school. They had about fifteen minutes left before the game against the Palisades Pumas got under way.

"The cheers *are* getting a little old, guys," said Maria Santelli, taking Jessica's side. "It feels like we do the same things over and over again."

"Look, it's fine with me if that's what everyone else wants. Just tell me what we should be doing differently, and we can all vote on it," Robin said.

"Let's see who can think up the best new cheer," Jessica said, her eyes brightening. Of course, she had already decided *she* would be the one to come up with the best cheer. "Then we can surprise everyone with it at the Big Mesa game in two weeks!"

"That's a great idea," Amy declared.

Robin shrugged. "OK. But I still don't see what's wrong with the ones we've got. I happen to like the pyramid," she added stubbornly.

Jessica ignored her. "Let's make it a contest. We can see who comes up with the best new cheer between now and the Big Mesa game." Her mind was already racing, trying to think of something that would show herself off to best advantage.

They took a quick vote, and it was decided to go ahead with Jessica's idea.

For the first time in days Jessica felt good again about cheerleading. The truth was, she had a private reason for wanting a new cheer that would really get everyone's attention. She'd been noticing Danny Porter a lot lately. Not only was Danny the wide receiver for the Gladiators, but he had an incredibly cute smile and the most heartbreakingly blue eyes. Danny was definitely crush material, but he was unbelievably shy. He almost never dated, and Jessica wasn't doing very well trying to get his attention.

She wasn't about to explain all this to Robin, but she had a feeling that an exciting new cheer might get Danny to take more notice of her. It would be the perfect ice-breaker. Jessica was sure she could bring up the subject of the cheer around Danny—somehow make sure he saw her perform it—and then she could modestly admit that she was the one who'd made it up.

Danny would turn those gorgeous blue eyes her way, and that would be that, she just knew it! So all she needed now was the perfect cheer. Even if it took all her ingenuity, Jessica was confident this was one contest she was going to win.

Jessica was in an especially good mood after the Palisades game. Sweet Valley had beaten the Pumas solidly, 21–9, and Scott had been carried off the field in a blaze of glory. But not before Jessica managed to get over to Danny Porter and pat him on the shoulder!

"Good going, Danny," she said in her most flirtatious voice.

41

Danny blushed and gave her an embarrassed smile, and Jessica was on cloud nine.

That was when she caught sight of Claire Middleton, sitting by herself on the bleachers and watching the players head off toward the locker room.

Jessica didn't really know anything about Claire, but she and Amy had decided to use her to prove that Pi Beta Alpha wasn't as snobby as people thought. Personally, she didn't see what was so bad about being a little exclusive, but she didn't want the sorority to get in trouble for it. Maybe if they invited the new girl to join, people who'd been giving them a hard time would change their opinions about Pi Beta Alpha.

Jessica had been looking for an opportunity to approach the new girl, and this seemed like the perfect time.

"Claire!" she called, hurrying over to join her.

Claire looked up, surprised.

"Hi. I'm Jessica. Jessica Wakefield. You haven't met me yet." Jessica made it sound as if Claire had been missing out on something wonderful.

"Nice to meet you," Claire mumbled.

Jessica felt a little put off. Claire didn't seem the least bit happy to meet her. Jessica looked her over. Up close Claire wasn't quite as much "Pi Beta Alpha" as she'd thought from a distance. Why was she wearing that shapeless T-shirt and those baggy jeans? Jessica decided to try to find out more about Claire.

"Great game, huh?" she said brightly.

"Yeah. But our defense looked a little weak. The linebacker blitz was causing some pretty big holes downfield."

Jessica stared at her. Football to Jessica was a bunch of cute guys rushing around wearing uniforms. Who knew anything about a line-backer blitz?

"You sound like you really know your stuff," Jessica said. Her tone was half-admiring, half-puzzled.

"Yeah, well, I'm pretty obsessive about foot-ball." Claire looked critically at Jessica's cheer-leading uniform. The disdain on Claire's face was obvious. "Don't you think being a cheer-leader is just a little bit sexist?" she blurted out. "After all, it's just a bunch of girls prancing around in cute little costumes."

Jessica stared at Claire. No one spoke to Jes-sica Wakefield like that. All thoughts of inviting Claire to join Pi Beta Alpha vanished from Jessi-ca's mind. What was wrong with Claire, she wondered. Maybe *she* didn't want to be a cheer-leader, but that didn't give her the right to be so critical.

"We happen to work very hard. And it's not sexist. We never said boys couldn't join," Jes-sica retorted. "Cheerleading is a lot more than just wearing our uniforms, for your information."

Claire shrugged but didn't even bother to look at Jessica. "Suit yourself. I think you'd do yourselves and everyone else a lot more good if you played a sport instead of jumping around and screaming."

Jessica was stung. Jumping around . . . and screaming? That was the way Claire described being a cheerleader?

"Well, thanks for the advice," Jessica said icily. She spun on her heel and marched away without another word. She couldn't believe she'd even thought once about asking Claire to join her sorority. What a bad-mannered, obnoxious girl she was.

Jessica had intended to offer Claire all her support in getting adjusted to Sweet Valley High. Well, she could forget that now. As far as Jessica was concerned, Claire Middleton had just made herself an enemy.

Four

Terri was running late Monday morning. First the blouse she wanted to wear wasn't ironed, and nothing else she tried on looked right. Next she couldn't find her sunglasses. Then she had to search for her math homework, and by the time she was finally out the door, she had missed the school bus.

"What a start to the week," she grumbled to herself, setting off on foot in the direction of the high school.

At least it was a gorgeous day. Birds were singing, the sky was perfectly blue, and the sun was so warm that her spirits started to lift, despite herself. She couldn't help looking forward to a new school week, and she was determined that this one would be wonderful. Coach Schultz was posting the sign-up list for quarter-

45

back tryouts that morning, and tryouts would start that afternoon, out on the playing field. Terri was going to be an instrumental part of them, marking down sprint times, passes thrown . . .

She had done a lot of thinking about the tryouts, and she was determined to be optimistic for Ken's sake. If he wanted to be quarterback again, she wanted that for him, too! Maybe she was just being paranoid about his eyesight. Surely Ken wouldn't make such an important decision without consulting his doctor. One thing was for sure: Ken needed her support in this, and if that meant suppressing her worries for a little while, then she would.

She entered the school building feeling better than she had all weekend. In fact, her good mood lasted all morning long. She answered three questions right in math class and even got a smile out of Jessica Wakefield when she made a witty comment as she passed her in the hall.

She could hardly wait to see Ken. They had a special place in the hallway where they usually met between third and fourth period classes, just before the turn she took to get to music and the room where he had his next class. Terri hummed as she walked quickly to their meeting place, but to her surprise Ken wasn't there.

Oh, well. He's probably late from his last class, she reasoned.

A minute later the first bell rang, signaling that class would start in three minutes. Ken still hadn't shown up.

Terri took one last look down the hall, then headed around the corner. She had no choice but to go on to music. She didn't want to be late. But it was a little disappointing, especially since she'd been so looking forward to sharing her new enthusiasm with Ken.

A nagging little voice inside her said, *Two or three weeks ago, Ken would have been here waiting for you—you know it. And now he's too busy doing something else.* But Terri straightened her shoulders, determined to shake off her uneasiness. Big deal—she'd see him at lunch. They were each other's best friends. They didn't have to meet at an appointed time for that to be true.

"Hey, have you seen the sign-up sheet yet?"

Terri looked up from her lunch as John Pfeifer sat down next to her.

"The coach put it up at eleven-thirty," John went on, "and there's already a good turnout. A couple of guys from the J.V. team are trying out—Dave Pollock and Stan Skinner, I think. Maybe one other guy."

Terri took a bite of her sandwich. "Good. I'm glad there's a lot of interest," she said.

"And you know whose name is first on the list, don't you?" John continued.

Terri looked up expectantly, but she was pretty sure she knew.

"Ken's!" John said, grinning.

"Great!" Terri exclaimed. "I had a feeling he was going to sign up!" She was genuinely excited, and proud of him, too.

"Can you imagine what a great story this is going to make in *The Oracle*? I can see it now. We'll call it 'The Comeback of a Quarterback.' Or maybe 'A Hero Returns.' "

Terri wiped her mouth with her napkin. "Don't start putting pressure on him, John," she cautioned. "What matters is that he tries his hardest. He doesn't need to prove to anyone that he's a hero."

John pushed his tray back and grinned. "Come on, Terri! He's a shoo-in! You know how much better he is than any of those J.V. guys. He'll be as good as he ever was. Maybe better. You know, I read this great story once in *Sports Weekly* about an ice hockey player who was temporarily blinded. He claimed when he came back he could play much better because his other senses had sharpened up so much when he couldn't see."

Terri finished her sandwich. "When does the coach take the list down? I want to go check it out," she said.

John looked at his watch. "I think the sign-up period ends at the end of lunch hour."

Terri stood and picked up her lunch bag. "See you," she called, heading for the door.

She scanned the hallway for Ken as she made her way to the locker room. Wanting to see the coach's list was only part of the reason she'd left the cafeteria early. The fact was, she wanted to find Ken. After missing him that morning, and now at lunch, too, she felt a little left out of his big decision. She wanted to be reassured that everything between them was all right.

It was twelve-thirty-five when Terri reached the door to the boys' locker room, where Coach Schultz had posted the sign-up list.

Just as John had told her, there was a long list of would-be quarterbacks. Terri recognized several of the names from the junior varsity squad. Tim Nelson, one of the defensive players, had also signed up, which wasn't surprising, considering he'd always mentioned it would be fun to be a quarterback.

And there, right on top of the list, was Ken's name, written in strong, bold print.

Just as Terri was leaning closer for a better look, the door to the boys' locker room opened, and Coach Schultz stepped out. "Well, hello there, Terri. Nice list of candidates we've gotten here, isn't it? I think the tryouts this afternoon will be exciting."

Terri nodded. "I think so, too."

"You must be awfully proud of that boy-friend of yours. Not many young men would show so much resilience and determination. I know I'm proud of him," the coach continued as he reached for the list and took it down.

Terri smiled. "Me, too," she said.

"Coach Schultz, wait a second!"

Terri and the coach both turned at the urgent-sounding feminine voice behind them.

It was Claire Middleton, red in the face and out of breath from running. "I'm sorry," Claire panted. "I had to stay after in my lab class and couldn't get away . . . I had this experiment to finish . . . and I wanted to get here . . . before you took down the list." She stopped, trying to catch her breath.

The coach looked at her with surprise. "Why?" he asked.

Claire pushed her long, dark hair back from her face. "Because I want to add my name to it." She glanced up at the clock. "I'm not too late, am I?"

The coach stared at her. "No, you're not too late," he said, a confused look on his face. "Sign-up time doesn't end for another few min-utes. But I'm afraid I don't understand. Are you signing up somebody else? A friend of yours?"

"No. I want to sign up myself," Claire said.

She had caught her breath by now and sounded more composed.

The coach laughed. "Come on, now," he said pleasantly. "You haven't been at Sweet Valley High very long, have you?"

"I *am* fairly new here," Claire said calmly. "But I've had a chance to look over some of the school regulations, and I know there's nothing to prevent a girl from trying out for any team she chooses. You don't have to pick me for the position—not unless I'm the best."

Coach Schultz stared at Claire in amazement. "You're serious, aren't you?" he asked slowly.

"Yes," Claire replied. "And I'm good," she added matter-of-factly. "If there was a team for girls, I'd try out for that. But there isn't. And just because I'm a girl doesn't mean I should be discriminated against. I love football, Coach. All I want is the chance to try."

Claire spoke in an earnest, determined voice, and Terri had to admit she was impressed.

The coach scratched his head, and Terri thought he looked more confused than ever. "Well, I'll have to talk this over with Mr. Cooper and look up the rules," he mumbled. "I can't say right now that I remember anything specific about this. I mean, to tell you the truth, it just hasn't ever come up before. But the risk of injuries . . . this isn't badminton,

51

Claire. We're talking about tackle football—with boys who weigh an average of fifty pounds more than you."

Claire shrugged. "A good quarterback doesn't have to worry about being tackled. The position emphasizes speed, agility, and smarts. Look, all I'm asking is that you let me try. You're the one to decide if I'm any good."

"OK," Coach Schultz said. "I'll talk it over with Mr. Cooper and double-check what the rule books say. If there's no rule against it, you're welcome to try out." He shook his head. "But I have to warn you: Don't expect the others to be very happy about this. You're probably going to be in for some teasing."

"I don't care about that," Claire said firmly. The coach handed her the list, and she added her name to it, underlining it once for emphasis before giving it back to him.

Terri watched as Claire headed off down the hall. Just wait until she told Ken and John and Zack and the others that Claire Middleton was trying out for quarterback of the Sweet Valley High Gladiators! It looked like routine scrimmages were going to be anything but routine!

By mid-afternoon the whole school was buzzing with the news about Claire. Zack and John already knew about it by the time Terri caught up with them in study hall. But she didn't see Ken until history class.

"Where have you been?" she whispered as she slid into her usual seat next to Ken's.

He leaned over and gave her an apologetic look. "I had to go over some medical forms in the nurse's office this morning. And I had an appointment with Dr. Cragie at lunch that I'd completely forgotten about. My mom called the principal's office to remind me. Sorry I missed you," he added.

"Me, too," Terri said. Ken smiled at her, and she felt at once as though things were back to normal.

"Guess what? The good news is, Dr. Cragie thinks there's no reason I can't try out for quarterback. He says my vision is close to one hundred percent restored!"

"That's great!" Terri said. She heaved a big sigh of relief. That was one less thing to worry about. It looked as though everything was going to be all right, after all.

Mr. Jaworski was standing up in front of the room, and Terri knew she wouldn't have a chance to talk to Ken again until after class. But she couldn't resist passing him a note that read, "Did you hear about your competition?"

Ken read it with a smile. "Yeah—pretty interesting, huh?" he scribbled back.

"Do you think she's crazy, or is she just trying to pull the coach's leg?" Terri wrote.

She thought she saw Ken frown as he read her question. He paused for a second, then wrote back, "No, I think she's serious. Who knows? Maybe she'll be good. We'll see this afternoon."

Mr. Jaworski cleared his throat, and when Terri glanced up, he was looking straight at her with a stern expression. "Excuse me, Miss Adams. Can we trouble you to share what you're writing with the rest of the class?"

Everyone giggled, and Terri could feel herself turning beet red. "Uh—no, sir. I mean . . . I'm sorry." She shoved Ken's note into her pocket and sat straight up.

"Try to pay attention, please," Mr. Jaworski said to the class at large. "I know you all have a lot of things on your minds that may seem more important than history. But trust me, the French Revolution seemed pretty important at the time."

Everyone laughed. History class resumed, but Terri couldn't concentrate. All she could think about was the tryouts that would start in less than an hour. Ken didn't seem at all shocked that Claire was trying out for the team. It just went to show how open and accepting he was. Most guys in his position would ridicule Claire. But not Ken, she thought proudly.

Terri admired Claire, too. It must have taken a lot of guts to decide to do something as daring as trying out for the football team. Terri knew more about football than most of the other girls at school put together, but she had never once considered something like that. It was partly because she liked the math and strategy behind the game more than the athletics of it, Terri supposed. And she didn't delude herself about being strong enough or quick enough to compete with the other players.

She hoped Claire had what it took to be a strong competitor—but not strong enough to beat Ken!

Five

Jessica scowled as she tried to fasten the skirt of her cheerleading costume with a safety pin, working the pin into the place where her button had fallen off. Over the weekend she had tried to think of a great cheer for their competition, but nothing very good had come to mind. If only she could come up with something really new and shocking . . .

She looked up as the door to the girls' locker room burst open and Amy Sutton rushed in.

"Can you believe that Claire Middleton is trying out for quarterback?" Amy's gray eyes were wide with amazement. "Isn't that the most ridiculous thing you've ever heard?"

Jessica was dumbfounded. "What?" she gasped.

"Don't tell me you haven't heard yet," Amy

said. "Where have you been, Jess? The whole school's been talking about nothing else all afternoon." She slipped off her jacket and started changing into her red-and-white skirt and white sweater. "Apparently the coach has been in meetings all afternoon with Chrome Dome Cooper. They're trying to figure out if there's some rule they can use to keep her from doing it."

"She's out of her mind," Jessica muttered, turning her attention back to her skirt. "What if Tad Johnson tackles her?" she added with a giggle. Tad "Blubber" Johnson, Zack Johnson's older brother, was the heaviest senior on the team. He weighed over two hundred pounds.

"She probably won't make it through the first scrimmage," Amy said, lacing up her tennis shoes.

Jessica frowned. She wasn't sure what she believed on principle about a girl trying out for football, but the fact that it was Claire Middleton made up her mind for her. She was still furious about the rude way Claire had treated her after Saturday's game. "I think she's showing off," Jessica pronounced. "She's obviously just trying to get attention," she added, smiling mischievously as an idea came to her. "And I know just how to put her in the spotlight."

"What do you mean?" Amy hurried to catch

up with Jessica as she crossed the locker room to the exit door.

Jessica gave Amy a conspiratorial smile. "Only that, personally, I'd be more than happy to make sure that Claire gets all the attention she deserves!"

Usually tryouts were sparsely attended, with just a handful of friends who came to cheer their favorites. But that afternoon, in addition to the entire football team, a few dozen students sat in the bleachers to watch the preliminary exercises. Terri looked up from the table where she was sitting, which had been set up near the bleachers and contained water bottles, stat sheets, and a few stopwatches. The entire *Oracle* staff was there, including John Pfeifer and Elizabeth Wakefield. Terri was pleased to see that Winston Egbert and a whole group of Ken's friends had shown up, too, and were sitting near the sidelines.

Coach Schultz strolled out onto the field and looked at his clipbboard. One by one he read the names of the people trying out for quarterback. Ken Matthews was first. Next came three boys from the junior varsity team: Stan Skinner, Dave Pollock, and Patrick Reeve. Tim Nelson, the linebacker, was fifth on the list, and after him were two other varsity players: Robbie Hendricks and Bryce Fisherman. Claire Middleton was last.

After the coach had called out all eight names, he assembled the group in a huddle not far from the table where Terri sat.

"Everybody ready?" he asked.

Terri saw Robbie Hendricks roll his eyes and look across the huddle to where Claire was standing. "Come on, Coach. You can't mean you're really going to let her try out."

The coach frowned at him.

"Now, listen up, guys," he said, his eyes flickering around the circle. "I've been through this thoroughly with Mr. Cooper. We've covered the rule books from A to Z, and there's nothing that says Claire can't try out for the football team if she wants to. Under the sexual discrimination code, we're allowed to have a separate team for boys, but we're not allowed to forbid a girl from trying out for it. Do you understand that?"

Terri noticed that all seven boys looked at each other. A few grumbled but didn't say anything. Claire stood silently, staring down at the ground.

"Fine," Coach Schultz said. "Now, before we even get started, I want you to know that we're losing the most important member of our team. Scott's done a wonderful job, but he's not going to be able to play for the rest of the semester.

And since Ricky Ordway is out with an injured hamstring, as you all know, he can't take over Scott's spot. So, we're going to need two quarterbacks: first and second string." He frowned before continuing. "I don't think I need to remind any of you that our record so far this season is ten wins, two losses. That ties us with Big Mesa for first place in our division. We're a team of winners, and unless every single one of you is a winner, I want you to leave the field right now." Everyone stared at him unblinkingly, and he nodded. "Good. Then I guess we can get started.

"Today we're going to try to get some sense of your speed." The coach waved to Terri, and she hurried over.

"Terri Adams is the number-cruncher for this team, as some of you already know. She's going to be helping me keep track of your times this afternoon. After some sprints and relay races, we'll try a few passes. Then we'll go through some of the team's regular warm-up and practice exercises: grass drills, wind sprints, running bleacher stairs. Terri and I will be watching you, taking notes on your condition. And remember, the Gladiators win because we're team players.

"Don't try any star stuff here. We want you to work *with* each other, not try to trip each other up."

Claire seemed to be hanging on every word the coach said. Her long hair was pulled back in a rubber band, and her usually pale face was suffused with color. Claire looked in pretty good shape, from what Terri could see. Her body was lithe and fit in her gray sweat shorts, and she moved with such grace and agility, it looked as if she was dancing, even when she was just loping after the others. Plus she had a firm, athletic look that Terri had always admired, with smooth, defined muscles in her upper arms, thighs, and calves.

Practice got off to its usual rigorous start. Coach Schultz had all eight candidates run a series of bleacher steps. Next he asked them to line up on the grass and run in place, fast, for several minutes, alternately diving down onto the grass to do push-ups, then bouncing back up to run in place. Those exercises, called ups and downs, were dreaded by the entire team. Both Stan Skinner and Dave Pollock dropped back and fell on the grass, panting. Claire didn't miss a beat, and neither did Ken.

"OK, let's try timing a forty-yard sprint," Coach Schultz said when the preliminary warmups were completed.

Terri took up her position at the finish line and held her stopwatch ready. The coach wanted the contestants to run in alphabetical order, so Bryce Fisherman was first, then Robbie Hendricks. Both made fairly good times. Next came Ken. Terri felt herself holding her breath as he crouched down, waited for the whistle, then sprang into a run. Four point nine seconds!

Ken's friends roared and whistled in the bleachers. "Yeah, Ken! Way to go, Matthews!" He'd beaten the others by a good three seconds and was in the lead.

Claire Middleton was next. She walked to the starting line, and Terri saw a look of intense concentration come over Claire's face.

"This is a football team! No girls allowed!" someone jeered from the stands.

Terri was glad to see that Claire had support, as well. Dana Larson, who had been extremely vocal in recent weeks about the lack of funding and attention given to girls' sports, stood up and yelled, "Show 'em your stuff, Claire! Don't let them intimidate you!"

Claire didn't seem to notice any of the attention she was getting. She stood completely motionless, her eyes fixed on the end-line marker forty yards ahead.

Terri set her stopwatch and nodded to the coach, signaling that she was ready. Claire crouched down, her jaw set, her eyes blazing. Like a shot, she was off with the whistle, her long ponytail streaming behind her. Terri couldn't believe her eyes. She didn't think she had ever seen a girl run so fast! She clicked the stopwatch off as Claire crossed the forty-yard marker, and when she looked down, she could hardly believe the time. "Four point eight," she called shakily to the coach.

Claire made a faint grimace. She didn't say anything, but Terri got the distinct feeling she wasn't pleased.

"Way to go, Middleton," Ken said admiringly as Claire walked back to the starting line.

Claire shrugged her shoulders. "It was OK," she said indifferently, then turned to watch as Tim Nelson took his position.

Terri stared at her. OK? Claire's time had been great! Terri couldn't believe how modest Claire was being about it. But maybe that was just her style. Quiet, even withdrawn.

Ten minutes later the first sprint race was over, and Claire Middleton was leading the pack. Terri could hear the buzz of comments from the small groups gathered in the bleachers. Obviously they were just as impressed as she was by how fast Claire had run.

John Pfeifer and Elizabeth Wakefield came down to join Terri.

"She's amazing!" John exclaimed. "I've got to tell you the truth. I thought she was insane, coming out here this afternoon. But she ran like crazy!"

Elizabeth was brimming with excitement. "She's terrific! Don't you think so, Ter?"

Terri laughed. "Yeah, she was pretty great," she agreed, looking back over her shoulder to the playing field.

The players were taking a fifteen-minute break before the next trial, and Terri was hoping Ken would come over. The tryouts had been incredibly exciting—especially since the forty-yard dash—and she was dying to go over everything with him. So far he was doing extremely well, but so was Claire. That had to be hard on his ego.

She smiled as Ken hastened over to the table to grab a quick drink of water from the cooler. "Hey, Ter!" he said, leaning over to rumple her hair. His face was so flushed with excitement and high spirits that Terri couldn't help but feel happy for him. He looked as if he was having the time of his life.

"Hi!" she said warmly, grinning up at him. "You're looking pretty good out there, you know that?"

"You think so?" Ken said happily.

"You look great," John chimed in.

Ken took a deep swig of water. "It feels really good to be out here again," he said. "Hey, pretty strong people we've got trying out, don't you think?" he added, smiling at Terri.

Terri felt a rush of warmth spread through her. That was so characteristic of Ken, she

64

thought. He was always so supportive of other people.

"Yeah, they do look good," she agreed. "Claire's a fast runner, isn't she?"

"She sure is." Ken let out a low whistle. "Boy, I wouldn't mind being able to run forty yards in that time. And she wasn't even happy with it! I wonder what she does on a good day."

"She's amazing," John agreed. "And she doesn't look the slightest bit ruffled by the hecklers."

Elizabeth nodded. "She's obviously got a lot of poise."

"You're right, Liz," said Ken. "She acts like a real pro. To tell you the truth, I think she looks pretty good out there."

"And she's cute, too," John added.

Ken laughed. "You've got that right. The team could use someone with her looks."

Terri shot a sideways glance at Ken. It wasn't like him to compliment another girl—not in front of his girlfriend, anyway.

"She has a lot of guts, too," Ken went on, "trying out in front of all these clowns. Truth is, I wish her a lot of luck."

"Hey, you'd better get back out there," Elizabeth said suddenly. "The coach is waving at you."

Ken set down his cup of water and gave Terri

a quick kiss. "Hey, wish me luck!" he said. "I'm going to need it. My passing arm's pretty rusty."

Terri watched him turn and jog lightly back to the spot on the field where the coach and the other candidates for quarterback were standing around. His comment about Claire hadn't meant anything, Terri told herself. He was just being a good sport.

But a few minutes later, when Ken loped over to the spot where Claire was stretching out on the grass and gave Claire the thumbs-up sign, Terri felt tears stinging her eyes. Could she really be losing Ken after all?

Six

"Hey, Ter!" John Pfeifer called, catching up to Terri on her way out to the playing field on Tuesday afternoon. "Wait up a second!"

He was out of breath, and his face was flushed. "I can't wait to see what happens today. I got a call from the sports editor at the *Sweet Valley News,* and they want to do a special on Ken and Claire Middleton. This is turning into a real media attraction!"

It was unusual for the local paper to cover high school tryouts, although they always covered the games.

Terri laughed. "I'm not surprised they'd be interested," she told him. "I heard the coach say that Claire's the first girl to try out for quarterback in any public high school in the whole area. She's big news."

Big news was an understatement, Terri thought. It was already clear that Ken and Claire were in the lead. Claire seemed to have the edge on Ken when it came to speed, but Ken was better at throwing. Both seemed to be doing fairly well at strategy and calling plays. The other candidates had dropped back, with Dave Pollock running a distant third behind Ken and Claire.

Reactions to Claire's performance were very mixed among the students at Sweet Valley. Dana Larson and Elizabeth Wakefield were strongly behind her, and they had managed to drum up a number of others—boys as well as girls—who supported Claire. But there was still a large, and vocal, majority against her. It was not surprising that some of the more immature and chauvinistic boys were loudest in putting Claire down, but Terri was disappointed at how many girls had complained that Claire was being "unfeminine."

Given her position on the team—and the fact that she and Ken were a couple—Terri had been in the midst of every debate about Claire. The controversy was pretty exciting, although it did take up a lot of time and energy.

The night before, she had been so keyed up she could hardly eat dinner. Her little brother, Mark, of course, had heard all about Claire from his best friend, Dean, Stan Skinner's little brother.

"I can't believe Ken's trying out against a

girl," Mark had muttered through a mouthful of hamburger.

That had gotten her parents' attention. "A girl? Trying out for the football team?" her father asked curiously.

She had already spent a long day going over and over all of this at school. But of course Mark and her parents had wanted to hear every detail—and they weren't the only ones. All evening the phone kept ringing—friends from school, guys on the team, even the reporters from the *News*, who wanted to confirm some of the race times she had recorded that afternoon.

Usually Terri enjoyed talking shop with everyone. But she'd been hoping to call Ken to discuss the trials, and with all the other calls there simply hadn't been time.

It had been great seeing Ken back out on the football field. Terri sincerely hoped he would make quarterback, and it certainly looked as if he had a good chance. But the tryouts—and all the attention Claire was getting—were straining her relationship with Ken, and she was looking forward to the time when they would be over so things could go back to normal. It wasn't the most loyal spirit, but she couldn't help it.

Maybe today's tryouts would help pick her up, Terri thought, as she scanned the field. Her eyes lit up when she spotted Ken doing some stretches. She hadn't even had a chance to talk to him in history class. She hoped they would be able to spend some time together after tryouts. She really missed him.

Suddenly John let out a low whistle.

Turning, Terri saw Claire jog out of the girls' locker room and onto the field.

"Look at that!" John exclaimed. "Have you ever seen a football uniform with that much style?"

Terri followed Claire's progress toward the field. Today her dark hair was pulled back with a stretchy terry cloth band, and her white sweatshirt made her complexion glow. The slight padding she wore made her seem slimmer than ever, and even more graceful.

Idiot, Terri scolded herself. *Why should you care what Claire looks like . . . or what John thinks of her, unless—*

That was when the truth hit her: She was intensely jealous of Claire.

Terri glanced back to where Ken stood on the field. Terri winced when she saw him give Claire a big smile as she approached. Claire said something to Ken that Terri couldn't hear and dropped down on the grass to stretch beside him. Ken laughed and gave her a playful punch on the shoulder.

Coach Schultz blew his whistle. "Everybody, line up!" He waved Terri over, then explained, "This afternoon I want to see some teamwork.

70

This isn't an easy quality to assess, but what I've decided to do is break you down into pairs for the afternoon and watch the way you work together—passing, running, receiving, calling plays." He consulted his clipboard. "Ken, you'll be partners with Claire. Tim, you'll work with Dave Pollock, Robbie, you'll be with Bryce. And Stan and Patrick can team up."

Terri bit her lip. So Ken and Claire were a team now. She hated herself for feeling the way she did. It was stupid and completely unfounded. Ken had every reason to be friendly with Claire. It was perfectly natural for him to be warm and cooperative. Why did she have to feel so jealous all of a sudden, just because Ken happened to be trying out with a girl?

"All right, partner," Terri heard Ken say as he turned to Claire and put out his hand.

John came up beside Terri then. "Lucky Ken," he commented. "It must be much more fun to practice teamsmanship with Claire than with Stan or Dave!"

Terri looked away. She could feel her face redden. It was just a teasing comment—John hadn't meant anything by it—but it only made her feel worse.

She tried to reason with herself. Her being jealous of Claire was her own problem, not Ken's. They had a wonderful relationship. But there was one nagging fear that Terri couldn't get out of her mind: She and Ken had fallen in love when Ken was blind, when he needed her. Back in the days before the accident, Ken hadn't even really noticed her. And deep down, irrational as it was, Terri was afraid that regaining his sight and his old life might mean that Ken would lose something else—his love for her.

"See?" Elizabeth teased Todd. "I told you that our anonymous female quarterback would finally come forward."

"You were right," Todd said. "I have to admit, she's pretty impressive. But Ken looks good, too," he added.

Dana Larson, who was sitting beside them, could barely contain her excitement. "This is exactly what this school has needed for a long time. Maybe Claire will wake up our athletics department and make them realize that girls can be just as serious about sports as boys!"

Elizabeth nodded. "I think Claire's waking up a lot of us." She gestured toward a group of boys, mostly sophomores, who were watching Claire with utter amazement.

"Listen, when you did that interview with Claire, did she say anything about trying out for the team?" Dana asked Elizabeth.

Elizabeth shook her head, remembering how mysteriously Claire had behaved during Friday's interview. "No, and it's been kind of bothering me. She did get really excited when she talked about football. I tried to draw her out, but she was very reluctant to talk about it." She sighed. "The truth is, I didn't do a very good job of getting information out of her at all."

Penny Ayala was making her way up the bleachers toward them. "Liz! I need to talk to you!" she said, sitting down next to Elizabeth. "Can you believe this? Whoever would've guessed our new student would turn out to be the biggest news story of the year?" She shook her head. "I've had two more calls just today from the *Sweet Valley News*. Claire Middleton is hot stuff, huh?"

Elizabeth nodded. "I was just telling Todd how badly I feel that I didn't get more of a sense of this when I interviewed her," she said.

Penny nodded. "Well, actually, that's what I wanted to talk to you about. Given all the excitement, we were hoping you could revise your interview a little—add on to it. If you could try to talk to Claire after tryouts today and find out more about her decision to try out for the team, that would be wonderful."

"Sure, Penny. I don't know how much information I'll be able to come up with, but I'll try."

"Good." Penny smiled at her. "If anyone can

do some good, solid investigative reporting, it's you! See what you can come up with, Liz, and we'll talk tomorrow."

When tryouts were finished, Elizabeth went down to the field and approached Claire, who was toweling off her face.

"Hi, Claire. Do you mind if I just ask you a couple of questions?" Elizabeth asked pleasantly.

Claire turned to her, a frown on her face. "Questions? About what?"

"Well, that interview I did the other day . . . Penny Ayala, the paper's editor in chief, doesn't think it's really complete enough." Elizabeth got out her notepad. "Now that you've shocked the whole school by trying out for the team, we'd like to know a little bit more about your interest in football."

"Like what?" Claire asked. "I thought we already went over everything."

This wasn't going to be any easier than the last interview, Elizabeth thought. "Well, you didn't mention that you were planing on trying out for the team," she prodded gently. "Have you always wanted to try out for the Gladiators? Did you ever think about trying out for the team at your old school?"

Claire shrugged. "No one wants to hear about that kind of thing," she said bluntly. "There's nothing different about me. I'm just like any of the other students who are trying out. I just like to play football, that's all."

Elizabeth stifled a sigh of frustration. Claire was one of the most evasive people she had ever met! "Look, it may not seem out of the ordinary to *you*, but a lot of people are very curious about you. They want to know what's made you so interested in football—and so good at it. Did you ever have a mentor? Someone who helped train you? Did you play when you were younger, or—"

"To tell you the truth, I'm kind of tired, Elizabeth," Claire cut in. Elizabeth saw with dismay that the closed expression on Claire's face had changed to one of angry impatience. "I've had a long workout, and I really want to take a hot shower and relax a little bit. Sorry, but I don't have anything else to tell you. Like I said before, I'm not much fun to write about."

Elizabeth stared at her. "Well, if that's how you really feel . . ." she began uncertainly.

"It is. Thanks for understanding," Claire said abruptly. Without another word she spun around and walked off in the direction of the girls' locker room.

Elizabeth felt uncomfortable. Usually she was good at drawing people out, but she had sure managed to wreck this assignment. She couldn't understand why Claire had to be so close-mouthed about her desire to join the team.

Elizabeth still wanted to get to know Claire better. But Claire seemed intent on keeping her feelings strictly to herself.

Jessica did one last jump with her pom-poms and then sat down on the first row of the bleachers, her blue-green eyes sparkling. She was in a wonderful mood. She knew she had looked good during practice, and with tryouts going on, there had been more people than usual to see her. She had even managed to make eye contact with Danny Porter!

Jessica and the other cheerleaders were the last ones left on the field. They had managed to keep an eye on what was happening. Now they were rehashing the tryouts, discussing the pros and cons of each candidate.

"What do you think Claire's chances are?" Maria Santelli asked.

Amy Sutton made a face. "I think she's a disgrace to our sex, if you really want to know," she piped up.

"What do you mean, Amy?" Robin Wilson asked. "She's good. Why shouldn't she try out for the position?"

"She looks like a jerk, that's why," Amy said.

76

"I think she's kind of brave," Jeanie West said slowly.

"Me, too," Annie Whitman agreed.

Jessica had remained uncharacteristically quiet, sizing up where everyone stood on the issue of Claire Middleton. She knew she had Amy on her side. It was the others she needed to work on. Looking around the circle of faces, she now said, "Well, you guys are great to be so supportive. Too bad Claire doesn't feel that way about what *you* do."

"What do you mean?" Sandra Bacon demanded.

Jessica shrugged. "She just happened to tell me that she thinks cheerleading is a stupid waste of time, that's all."

Sandra and Jeanie stared at each other. "No way," Jeanie said, sounding upset.

"That's what she told me, anyway. I guess cheerleading is too traditional for someone like Claire." Jessica watched for the other cheerleaders' reactions and was glad to see that they looked irritated.

"That's really dumb," Amy said. "What does she want us to do instead? Try out for wrestling?"

The other girls giggled.

"It doesn't seem like a very fair attitude," Robin said slowly. "We support what she's doing. I wonder why she doesn't feel the same about us?"

77

"Because," Jessica cut in—she sensed that she was having just the effect she'd hoped for, and she wanted to make the most of it—"she thinks we're exploiting ourselves. 'Prancing around in cute little costumes' was the way she put it, I think."

Amy was furious. "I can't stand that girl!" she cried. "What right does she have judging us? She hasn't been here very long, but she already thinks she's God's gift!"

"Maybe she didn't mean to be so critical," Annie suggested uncertainly. "I guess if you're as serious about sports as she is, cheerleading must seem a little tame."

"It still isn't fair of her," Sandra objected. "We spend a lot of time practicing, and we really support the players. That ought to count for something. Besides, cheerleading's a sort of sport, too."

"I agree," Jeanie said firmly. "It's sexist to say a girl can't try out for a certain sport. But it's also sexist to say girls shouldn't do something they want to, like cheerleading."

Amy Sutton nodded. "You're right, Jeanie. To tell you the truth, I think there's something a little weird about 'Fair Claire.' "

Jessica's eyes brightened. "I like that . . . Fair Claire. Maybe we should think up some more rhymes for her." She flipped back her hair. "Or better yet, how about a personalized cheer, just for her?"

"Like what?" Amy demanded.

Jessica tried an experimental position. "Give us a clap," she tried, jumping to one side and clapping her hands. "Give us a twirl." The other cheerleaders looked on expectantly as Jessica thought hard.

Within seconds she had come up with the perfect personalized-for-Claire-Middleton cheer:

"Give us a clap!
Give us a twirl!
Give us a quarterback
who isn't a girl!"

Everyone burst out laughing.

"What a great idea!" Maria Santelli exclaimed. "You said you've been trying to think of a way to make the cheers more exciting, Jess. Well, why not come up with customized cheers for each player? That way we can let the guys know we're really making an effort for them."

"Yeah," Robin said. "It could be part of our contest for a new cheer. Let's each come up with one. Then we'll vote on the best one, and that's the one we'll start with. The Big Mesa game is a week from this Saturday, so let's choose by the middle of next week."

Jessica grinned triumphantly. She had to admit she *was* pleased with her cheer for Claire. And she knew she could do a lot better, too. Claire Middleton wasn't going to get away with dismissing cheerleading the way she had. Claire was going to learn about life at Sweet Valley the hard way. And the first lesson was going to be that Jessica Wakefield didn't let people put her down!

Seven

On Wednesday at lunch Terri found herself sitting at the same table as Elizabeth Wakefield. She and Elizabeth didn't spend a lot of time together, but Terri liked her a lot. Elizabeth had been incredibly perceptive and sympathetic right after Ken's accident, and Terri always felt comfortable around her.

"How's Ken feeling about the football tryouts?" Elizabeth asked. "Is he pleased with the way everything's going so far?"

"He seems to be," Terri said. "He's doing a wonderful job."

It was true. Ken was really happy about at how well he was doing. In fact, she didn't think she'd ever seen him so happy. She just wished she could feel the same way. . . .

Elizabeth nodded. "Yeah, he sure is." She

paused, fiddling with her straw. "It must be a little weird for you. After all, Ken isn't the only one who went through the agonies of losing and regaining his vision these past few months. You've been through a lot of it, too."

"I haven't been through anything!" Terri objected. "After all, I never had to face the stuff Ken did. I tried to understand how he was feeling, but I couldn't really come close." She shook her head. "If anything, Ken's blindness made me realize that people who don't have a physical handicap can never really understand what one is like."

"I didn't mean that you had to go through exactly what Ken did. I just meant that you've had your own troubles to go through, and this must be a weird time—wonderful in most ways, kind of difficult in others." Elizabeth smiled. "I'm just thinking about how I'd feel. A lot of people assume that once Ken began to recover, all the work was over. But I'd be willing to bet there's still a lot more to get through."

Terri nodded slowly. "You're right," she said. "The truth is, I haven't been feeling myself around Ken since—"

"Since when?"

"I guess since he decided to try out for quarterback," Terri admitted.

Elizabeth nodded. "I think I understand, Terri.

It's hard to keep adjusting as a relationship changes. I'd feel a lot like you do if Todd and I had gone through what you guys have."

"Really?" Terri felt a huge rush of relief. She'd been tormenting herself for being selfish, for looking back nostalgically to the time when Ken was blind. But Elizabeth's support made her feel a little less upset with herself. Elizabeth was right. Just because Ken could see again didn't mean the work was over. It was going to take time to get used to this new phase of their relationship, and Terri knew she shouldn't be so impatient with him—or with herself.

She and Ken had planned to have dinner together that night and then study at the library. It was the first time in over a week that they would be alone together, and Terri was determined to make it a fun evening. After talking with Elizabeth, she felt certain it would be.

It was Ken's idea to stop at the Dairi Burger before going to the library that night. Terri was a little disappointed. She had been hoping for someplace a little more private, but the Dairi Burger was convenient, and at least they shared a lot of great memories there!

They sat at their usual booth at the back, and within a few minutes Terri had relaxed and was actually enjoying herself. Ken was starving, even after two hamburgers, and she laughed as she teased him about his gargantuan appetite. It gave her a thrill just to look at him across the booth. He looked absolutely wonderful. His blond hair was bleached from the sun and caught the reflection of the lights, and his arms and face were tanned from all the time he'd been spending outside practicing. Best of all, he looked happy and at ease, just like the old Ken.

He had just ordered yet another burger when the door opened and Terri saw Claire Middleton walk in. Claire didn't look to the right or left. She walked straight to the counter and ordered some food. She had some library books with her, and while she was waiting for her food she glanced through one.

"Look, there's Claire," Ken said.

Terri looked up at the counter, silent.

"She's all by herself," Ken continued, looking concerned.

Terri knew the polite thing to do would be to invite Claire to join them, but she didn't say a word. *Please*, she silently asked Ken, *don't wreck our date. I haven't been alone with you in ages. Don't spoil it by asking Claire to join us.* She knew it was selfish, but she couldn't bear the thought of anything ruining their night alone together.

Ken wouldn't let up, however. "Let's ask her to come over and eat with us," he suggested.

Terri opened her mouth to protest, but Ken was already calling Claire's name and waving to her. "Come sit down!" he urged her, as if he wouldn't take no for an answer.

Terri slumped down in her seat, feeling her happiness ebb away. Wasn't Ken enjoying their date—just the two of them? Hadn't he missed her the way missed him? And it didn't help that Claire was the reason why Terri felt so miserable. The last thing Terri wanted was to have to make small talk with Claire right now. She would rather just get up and go to the library by herself!

Terri watched dejectedly as Claire paid for her food and came over to their table. "Thanks, but my mom's out in the car. I'm on my way to the library," she added as she put the food in a bag.

"Oh . . ." Ken looked disappointed. Then he added, "We're going to the library, too. We could take you . . ."

"No, thanks. My mom's right outside," Claire said quickly. She was as serious and intense as ever. "Maybe some other time. See you at practice tomorrow," she added in a quiet voice.

"Right," Ken said, grinning at her. "See you tomorrow."

Terri fiddled with her straw, her face flaming.

She didn't want to look Ken in the eye. Why had he been so insistent that Claire join them? And why mention that they were on their way to the library, too? Was he so eager to be with Claire that he just couldn't help himself?

Ken took a huge bite out of his third hamburger as he watched Claire head for the door. All he said was, "Too bad. I'd like to get to know her better. She's really interesting."

Terri's confusion was growing. Ken didn't even seem embarrassed or apologetic about his behavior. He didn't seem to think there was any reason why Claire shouldn't have joined them. It was as if their date didn't mean anything to him. Before football tryouts had started, they'd spent a lot of time alone together. Now they hardly ever saw each other.

Terri felt she should try to explain to Ken why she was upset, but she didn't know how to begin. How could she explain without accusing him, without behaving just like the sort of clinging girlfriend Ken had described the last time they had been at the Dairi Burger? She was fumbling for the right words when she glanced up and saw a stricken expression on Ken's face.

His eyes were screwed up, squinting, and for an instant he put his hands on his eyes, covering them. The next second he shook his head slightly and appeared to be OK again.

"Ken? Are you all right?" Terri asked anxiously. Since Ken's doctor had given him the go-ahead to try out, she had stopped worrying about his eyes, but now she was sure there was a problem.

"I'm . . . uh, I'm fine. Fine," he said slowly. He didn't look fine. He looked pale and confused and frightened.

"Is it your eyes? Did you black out?" she demanded.

Ken's expression darkened. "I'm fine, Terri," he repeated stiffly.

Terri finished her drink in silence. What had really happened? It was clear he wasn't going to tell her, and that hurt her.

But maybe he didn't want to tell her because he knew what she was thinking: that if his vision wasn't entirely better, he had absolutely no business trying out for quarterback again.

Thursday at lunchtime, Jessica threw her books in her locker, slammed the door shut, and headed to the cafeteria. She was really sick and tired of all the attention Claire Middleton was getting. It was bad enough that so many students at Sweet Valley High treated her as if she were some kind of hero. But that day she'd been the subject of a lead story in the sports section of the *Sweet Valley News*. The whole community was obsessed with her!

"I know she's just eating up all this attention," Jessica said, glowering at Lila and Amy, as she sat down at their table. "She's so cool and indifferent all the time, like she doesn't care if she's in the news or not. But I'm sure all that's just an act."

"I still can't believe she made that comment about cheerleaders," Lila said.

"It's all I can think about," Amy put in. "Frankly, I think we need to get back at her. Claire's the kind of girl who doesn't even notice when we give her the silent treatment. Maybe we need to make our message stronger."

"Yeah, you're right," Lila agreed. "She's in my English class, and you should see the way she snubs people. Especially guys. This morning Danny Porter was trying to talk to her, and—"

Jessica's eyebrows shot up. "What?" she snapped.

"I said, Danny Porter was trying to talk to her, and she totally ignored him. I couldn't believe how rude she was."

Jessica's face flamed. So much for Danny Porter's shyness! Well, if he was interested in someone like Claire, he could just forget about Jessica making a play for him!

"I agree with Amy," Jessica said coldly. "I

think Claire needs to be taught a lesson." She was looking idly around the cafeteria, deep in thought, when suddenly her gaze fell on Tim Nelson and Stan Skinner. "You know," she said quickly, leaning forward a little, "I bet some of the guys who've been pushed out of the lead for the quarterback spot might be willing to help us."

Amy followed her gaze. "You're right. Stan supposedly can't stand Claire. He thinks she has a giant ego. And Tim thinks any girl who wants to play football has something wrong with her."

"How well do you know Tim?" Jessica asked Amy.

"He's my lab partner in science," Amy replied.

"Well, do me a favor," Jessica said slowly. "If you can draft Tim, I'll take care of Stan. He can talk to Robbie Hendricks and Bryce Fisherman. I think having a few more people on the revenge squad might really help us at this point."

"What should I ask him to do?"

"Oh . . . just some pranks. Let him use his imagination. Just try to encourage him a little." Jessica snapped her fingers. "I've got it! Tell him that Claire's been telling people he's a lousy player and shouldn't even be trying out. That sort of thing."

"Jessica!" Lila exclaimed. "Is that true?"

Jessica shrugged. "More or less," she fibbed.

She hadn't actually heard Claire say that, but after the way she had trashed cheerleading, Jessica could easily imagine her putting other people down, too. "Anyway, you know how literal guys are," she went on lightly. "You have to really goad them into doing something mean, especially to a girl."

Amy nodded. "You're right. I'll go to work on Tim right away. I'll convince him Claire needs to be taught a lesson."

"Good!" Jessica told her. "That's the spirit. I'll see what I can do with Stan. Between the four of us, we ought to be able to give Claire the message."

Lila shook her head. "All I can say is, I'd hate to be on your bad side, Jess," she murmured.

Jessica smiled serenely.

Terri made it to the locker room ten minutes early on Thursday afternoon. She had study hall last period that day, and she had finished her French homework ahead of time. Her plan was to change into sweats before tryouts, then maybe get some jogging in when tryouts were over. Not that she could ever be as athletic as Claire, but she liked feeling fit, and she had been neglecting exercise lately. Besides, she really needed to clear her head.

She was still concerned about what had happened the night before at the Dairi Burger. It was obvious that Ken's eyes had given him some trouble, and equally obvious that he wasn't going to talk about it. He'd gotten really mad at her when she tried to bring it up again at the library.

Maybe she should say something to someone else, Terri thought. After all, Ken's health could be at stake. But she knew he would never forgive her if she did. She just wished she knew what to do.

The locker room was empty, and Terri changed quickly. She was heading toward the back door, her gym shoes in one hand, when she heard a noise in the next row of lockers.

Claire was sitting all by herself on the bench, dressed in a pair of shorts and a sweatshirt. She had her back to Terri, and her head was in her hands. Her shoulders were shaking slightly, and it looked to Terri as if she was crying.

Terri paused for a moment, not sure whether to stop and say something or keep walking, but then she started into the row of lockers. Claire jumped up and spun around. Her gaze flew to Terri, then back to her open locker, where a large black-and-white photograph was taped up. In the photo a handsome boy in a football uniform was grinning out at the camera. "To Claire—with all my love, Ted," was scrawled across the bottom in blue ink.

Claire stared at Terri as if she were terrified, the color draining from her face. The next instant she slammed the locker shut, hard.

"I didn't hear you," she said in a shaky voice.

She *had* been crying, Terri realized. Her eyes were red, and her face was pale.

"Are you OK?" Terri asked her.

"I'm fine. I'm just . . . coach wanted . . . I'm supposed to be outside . . . I'm late," Claire stammered. She brushed her hair back from her face in a nervous gesture, and before Terri could say another word, she spun on her heel and fled.

Terri stared at the closed locker. The way Claire had slammed it shut, it was obvious she didn't want Terri looking inside. Was it because of the photograph of that football player?

Who was this guy Ted? she wondered.

Eight

When all of the candidates were assembled on the football field on Friday afternoon, Coach Schultz announced that there would be a special intrasquad game on Saturday morning, with defense squared off against offense. The new quarterback would be announced Monday morning.

That meant that by the end of today's tryouts, the two best players would be selected. Tomorrow morning the two quarterbacks would play against each other. That would give the coach a chance to see them in action.

After yesterday's practice, the coach had made some cuts. Tim Nelson was out, and so were Stan Skinner, Patrick Reeve, Robbie Hendricks, and Bryce Fisherman. That left Ken, Claire, and Dave Pollock in the running.

"We'll start today's trials in about ten minutes," the coach concluded. As he went over to discuss the following day's lineup with the rest of the team, Ken trotted over to where Terri and John Pfeifer were standing.

"You're bound to get it, Ken. Don't even pretend to be modest," John said cheerfully.

Ken shook his head. "I wouldn't be so sure of that. Believe it or not, Claire's beaten me in every race we've run. I may be a stronger passer than she is, but that girl runs like the wind."

Terri set her jaw. Why did Ken have to keep defending Claire and making her sound so great? He was supposed to be her competitor, not her biggest fan.

"Don't tell me you seriously think Coach Schultz is going to pick Claire Middleton to play against Peter Straus!" John shook his head vehemently. "No way. It's one thing to take her seriously here at Sweet Valley. But actually letting her play against a quarterback of Straus's strength and skill—it's impossible, Ken. You know that as well as I do." Peter Straus, the star quarterback of Big Mesa's team, was being recruited by many top college teams.

Ken shrugged. "All I'm saying is that tryouts aren't over yet."

Terri was relieved when John went to go sit in the bleachers and she and Ken were alone.

She felt so confused. She didn't know if she was just worried about Ken's eyes or jealous of Claire—or what. All she knew was she had been feeling pretty miserable lately and really needed to talk to him. But when she opened her mouth to say something, all the wrong words came out.

"Why have you been going out of your way to back Claire up?" she blurted.

Ken looked at her questioningly, and suddenly Terri felt incredibly foolish. What could she say? It *did* sound ridiculous. She didn't want to sound jealous and insecure.

"She needs support, Terri," Ken said, frowning. "I see the way some of the guys treat her, and it makes me sick. I want to help her in any way I can."

The emotion came through in his voice, and Terri felt a lump forming in her throat. Was Ken trying to say that he cared about Claire as more than a friend?

"Fine," Terri retorted. She turned abruptly and headed for the table where her stopwatch and clipboard were. She groaned when she realized Claire was standing right by the table, taking a drink of water. There was no way to avoid saying hello.

"Congratulations on making the cuts," Terri said in a flat voice.

Claire's jaw seemed to set. And she didn't look very happy. "I guess that's some compensation for the dumb pranks they've been pulling on me," she muttered.

"Pranks?" Terri asked. "What do you mean?"

"Oh, yesterday someone put toothpaste in the shoes I left in my locker, and I've gotten a couple of hate notes." She looked stonily at Terri. "I always bring a special vitamin drink to school for lunch, and someone swiped it today. It all adds up—those guys can't stand the thought that a girl can play football better than they can. They'll try anything to get back at me." She shrugged. "Who cares? They're just a bunch of jerks."

Terri didn't know which surprised her more, that these things had been happening or that Claire was confiding in her. "Doesn't it upset you?" she asked uncertainly.

"No." Claire's eyes flashed with determination. "I know what I want, and the last thing that would stop me is that kind of stupid trick."

Terri watched Claire closely. She didn't quite believe Claire when she said that the pranks hadn't bothered her. She might try hard to seem tough, but her voice had shaken a little when she described the notes she'd received. Of course it must hurt her, Terri realized. A person would have to be made of stone not to be affected.

But Terri's sympathy vanished the next minute.

"That's just another reason why Ken is so great," Claire said, bending over to lace up her shoes. "He's the only grown-up on the whole team. He's not afraid of competition. He's an incredible guy, Terri. You're really lucky to be with him, you know that?" She looked wistful. "He reminds me . . . he reminds me of someone really wonderful I used to know," she added softly.

Terri felt her stomach lurch. She could have sworn Claire's eyes had actually misted over. Claire was usually so controlled, but it was clear she felt strongly about Ken.

Terri bit her lip. She was certain that some kind of intense feeling had sprung up between Ken and Claire. They looked so happy when they talked about each other, and they'd only been spending every single afternoon together. Terri felt a sinking feeling in the pit of her stomach.

It was probably only a matter of time before Ken would break up with her so he could spend *all* his time with Claire.

Miserable as she felt, Terri forced herself to buckle down to her work. That day the coach had asked a number of team members to play defense, blocking and tackling the would-be quarterbacks as they tried to pass or run up the field to score touchdowns. After a few runs, it was clear to Terri that Ken and Claire were way ahead of Dave, in both running and passing. Claire darted in and out among the other players with astonishing agility. Her smallness was a real advantage as she dodged tackles, dove between bigger players, and leapt for the ball with the grace of a dancer. Ken also played well, with strength and speed that were better than ever. Dave just couldn't keep up—not with Claire, and not with Ken.

In the last couple of minutes of practice Ken was backing up to throw a long pass when he suddenly seemed to stumble. Terri gasped as she watched him grimace. He seemed to be in terrible pain! Then he tripped, dropped the ball, and tumbled to the ground.

Terri was about to run over to help him up, but before she moved, Ken was right back on his feet, snatching up the ball and throwing a perfect long pass to Danny Porter.

"You OK, Matthews?" the coach called, concerned.

"I'm fine," Ken called back.

But Terri wasn't so sure. She had seen the telltale gesture, the way Ken passed his hands—for just a fraction of a second—in front of his eyes to check his vision. Was he blacking out again? It frightened Terri, seeing him running around out there when she wasn't sure he was all better and ready to play. What if he hurt himself? She would never forgive herself. She had to try again to talk with him.

When tryouts wrapped up for the day, Coach Schultz announced that Ken Matthews and Claire Middleton would be the two quarterbacks in the next day's scrimmage.

There were still some people in the bleachers: Dana Larson, some of *The Oracle* staff, and a few others. Dana started a fanfare of applause for Claire, and Elizabeth joined in with her, crying, "Yeah, Claire!"

Terri was too preoccupied to pay them much attention, however. She waited anxiously for Ken at the sidelines.

"Listen, I'm really glad for you, but we have to talk," she said to him as he strolled up to her, unstrapping his helmet.

"I don't really feel like talking right now, Terri. Can't it wait till after tomorrow?"

From the look on his face Terri knew she'd been right. Something had gone wrong with his vision. "I can't let you go out on the field tomorrow if there's something wrong with your eyes!" she blurted out.

Ken glared at her. "Quit mothering me, Terri. That stuff was fine back when I needed it, but I can see just fine now. I don't need you playing nurse."

Terri stared at him, completely stunned. "I'm just trying to—"

"Trying to keep me from doing what I love," Ken finished bitterly. "You ought to be a little less protective, Terri. Take a lesson from Claire. Her motto is, 'I'd rather die than quit.'"

"Quit telling me how great Claire is all the time," Terri retorted, glaring back at him. "I'm sick and tired of hearing it. Claire wasn't there when you thought you couldn't even make it down the hallway without help!"

Ken backed up, his blue eyes filled with anger. "If you think a good relationship is based on gratitude, Terri, then you're crazy!"

"I don't know what a good relationship is based on," Terri shot back, hardly believing the words were coming out of her own mouth. "I just know that ours hasn't been very good lately!"

Just then, Claire walked over to them, a white towel draped around her shoulders. "Hey, congratulations, Ken," she said, holding out her hand to shake. "And may the best person win."

"You bet," Ken said, firmly gripping her hand. The stony anger on his face gave way to a smile. "Good luck tomorrow, Claire. Knock 'em dead." Then she walked away.

Terri looked away, her eyes brimming with unshed tears. "Ken, listen—" she began.

Ken shook his head. "You and I have to talk," he muttered. "But I can't do it now, Terri. Can't you see how much this means to me? Just let me be alone for a little while, OK? I need to think."

Terri watched him turn away. She could feel tears start to stream down her face. She had a horrible feeling that she knew what Ken meant by "You and I have to talk."

He was going to tell her that he didn't love her anymore and that he had fallen in love with Claire Middleton!

Terri was late getting back to the locker room. She'd had to help Coach Schultz go over the figures from the week of tryouts. By the time she finally opened the outside door to the locker room and slipped inside, it was mostly empty— empty enough so she could hear Jessica's and Amy's voices reverberating through the big room.

"She's driving me crazy. She's so smug about the whole thing." Amy's voice was strident. "It's not like she's just trying out for a position on a team, it's like she's a crusader or something. Well, I'm sick and tired of her. She's a snob, she's stuck up—and besides, Ken is the one who should be quarterback. There's no way I'm cheering at the Big Mesa game next week if Claire Middleton is quarterback."

"I can't believe Tim and those guys couldn't do a better job of scaring her off," Jessica added. "Who ever heard of such stupid tricks? Did you see them try to fill her helmet with water? When Coach Schultz came over, they had to pretend to be washing off her equipment."

"Yeah, they're so unimaginative." That sounded like Amy again. "Too bad. This means we're on our own, Jess. We'll have to think up something ourselves. Poor Claire, she doesn't even realize what she's up against. If we can't bring her to her knees, we deserve to have to cheer her on next Saturday."

Terri was still so upset about Ken that she was barely listening. She felt so desperate. She wished there was something she could do to keep her and Ken together. She had changed into her jeans and begun to brush her hair when the idea struck her. Amy and Jessica really had it in for Claire. And they needed a way to get back at her.

Well, maybe Terri could help them.

Five minutes later Terri was sitting on a locker room bench across from Jessica and Amy. The story she'd given them was plausible, and it made her sound pretty heroic, as if her desire to sabotage Claire's efforts came from being a loyal girlfriend.

"So that's why I want to help you guys," she finished. "Ken needs to be quarterback, and anything I can do to help him . . ." Terri let her voice trail off.

"I don't blame you. With all Ken's been through, it's terrible seeing him have to fight to get his old position back. And to have to fight someone like *Claire!*" Jessica declared.

Terri felt a twinge of guilt. After all, Claire had worked just as hard as Ken to get so far in the tryouts. But Terri pushed her uneasiness aside. After all, her relationship with Ken was on the line.

"So, Terri," Amy said. "Any ideas on how to get to Claire tomorrow? Something that will drive her away from the scrimmage—we want to make her quit."

Terri thought hard. "I talked to her today about some of those pranks the guys played on her. I think they bothered her, although she tried to hide it. She's pretty determined."

"Still, there must be something that would really upset her," Amy said.

Terri thought for a moment, then snapped her fingers. "I've got it!" she told them. "I know exactly what you guys ought to do!"

In seconds she had filled Amy and Jessica in on the scene that had taken place the previous afternoon. "I walked in and found Claire staring at this photo of a really cute guy in a football uniform. It was signed, 'To Claire—with all my love, Ted.' She freaked out when she saw me, like I'd caught her with stolen jewels or something, and then she slammed the door of her locker shut so I couldn't see inside."

"What are you saying? That we ought to mention this guy Ted in public? In front of Claire?" Amy asked doubtfully.

"I've got it!" Jessica cried. "We'll make up a little cheer, just for Claire, and we'll make sure it ends with something like . . . 'Who is Ted?'"

"I don't know," said Amy. "That sounds a little lame."

Jessica thought for a moment. "Then how about 'We know about Ted'?"

"Yeah," said Amy. "Something like that. We can work out the details later."

"It'll solve two problems," Jessica said. "We can win the cheerleading contest and humiliate Claire Middleton at the same time!"

"I'd love to show the world that she's as human as the rest of us," Amy admitted slowly.

Terri felt a little queasy. What had she done? She'd never schemed like this against someone before. Was she losing her mind?

But this was no time to question herself. She'd had it with being sensitive and keeping her feelings to herself. The world didn't reward people like that. The world rewarded fighters—like Claire.

Anyway, it was only a little prank. Whoever this Ted guy was, Claire shouldn't be so secretive about him. All they were going to do tomorrow was have some fun and tease her a a bit. If Claire took it the wrong way, well, that was her problem.

Nine

The scrimmage had gotten so much local publicity that it attracted a larger audience than many of the Gladiators' regular games.

Elizabeth got up early on Saturday morning, took a quick shower, and hurried downstairs. She was surprised to see Jessica already up and done with breakfast, intent on something she was scribbling on a piece of paper.

"What's that?" Elizabeth asked her.

Jessica folded the paper hastily. "Nothing. Just a little surprise cheer the cheerleaders are working on for today's scrimmage," she said.

Elizabeth looked at her suspiciously. "I know that look, Jess, and it usually means you're up to something. Come on. What is it?"

Jessica shrugged in response.

Seeing she couldn't get anything else out of her twin, Elizabeth changed the subject.

"Do you think Claire's going to pull this thing off and edge Ken out today?" she asked.

Jessica sighed dramatically. "Why does *every*-one give Claire so much attention? Just wait till after today. Once she realizes she isn't going to be quarterback, she won't be so full of herself all the time!"

Elizabeth took a sip of orange juice. "My sister the psychic," she teased. "How do you know Claire isn't going to be quarterback? Isn't that a little sexist of you?"

"I'm not sexist. I just happen to think it's ridiculous for a girl to try out for a boys' football team," Jessica snapped.

Elizabeth shook her head. "Why? Claire's good enough to have beaten out most of the competition so far. Why shouldn't she be allowed to play? If you ask *me*, we should consider ourselves lucky to have her around. I mean, maybe she'll end up winning the game for us against Big Mesa."

"That'll be the day," Jessica retorted. "Anyway, I don't have time to talk about this anymore. I've got to meet Amy." She grabbed the piece of paper she'd been writing on, and before Elizabeth could get another word in, Jessica raced out of the kitchen.

"What was that?"

Elizabeth's older brother, Steven, came in the side door from outside.

107

"Your little sister, en route to some kind of scheme or other, I'd guess." Elizabeth jumped up to give Steven a hug. "It's so good to see you! I didn't know you were coming home today. Do you and Cara have plans?"

Cara Walker, Steven's girlfriend, was a classmate of Elizabeth and Jessica's at Sweet Valley High, and Steven came down from the state university to spend time with her as often as he could.

Steven sat down and helped himself to a banana. "Well, I wanted to check out the football scrimmage. Cara told me all about this girl-wonder who's trying out for the Gladiators. I thought I'd come down and see what all the fuss is about."

Elizabeth took out the final draft of her interview with Claire, which she had promised Penny to have ready by Monday. "Well, you came at a good time. Help me think of a good way to describe this 'girl-wonder,' as you call her. I'm revising an interview with her for the school paper, and I'm just not sure how to close it. I don't want to sound too hopeful, since she may not make the team. On the other hand . . . well, I want to give her full credit for trying."

Steven got up and read over her shoulder. "Is that her name? Claire Middleton?" he asked curiously.

"Yeah," Elizabeth told him. "Is there something unusual about that?"

108

Steven shook his head. "No, nothing unusual." He was quiet for a minute. "You know, this may be a complete coincidence, but there was a guy in my freshman composition class named Middleton. He was a real football hero, too. I wonder . . ." He scratched his head. "Nah, there's no way. They couldn't be related. Too much of a coincidence for there to be that much football in one family."

"Maybe not," Elizabeth said. "Do you know where he's from?"

Steven shook his head. "It's a pretty horrible story, Liz. He was quarterback of our junior varsity team. They said he was destined for great things—supposedly he had offers from pro teams already, and he was only eighteen. Then he started having these terrible headaches. He was diagnosed with a brain tumor, and within a couple of months he was dead. I never knew him except by name, but my roommate was friends with him. He was really upset when he died—still talks about him all the time."

Elizabeth stared at him. "And his last name was Middleton?" she asked slowly.

Steven nodded. "Yeah, Ted Middleton."

Elizabeth fiddled with her pen, mulling over what her brother had just told her. "You know, maybe they *were* related. Maybe this guy Ted was her older brother. It would make sense, Steve." She filled him in on what had happened when she tried to ask Claire about her family background. "She was so defensive, it was clear I was intruding. I had the feeling I was trespassing on dangerous ground for her. Wouldn't that be a natural reaction if she'd had an older brother who died? An older brother who'd been her role model, who'd been the one who taught her to love football?"

Steven nodded. "And now that I think of it, my roommate did mention that the family moved to Sweet Valley after Ted's death."

"Then it must be her brother!" Elizabeth exclaimed.

She gathered her papers together. It all made sense: Claire's moodiness, her reluctance to talk. Her brother must have been the one behind Claire's intense desire to make the team.

Jessica ran up to Amy, her blond hair flying. "OK," she said. "I've got it. Can you get the rest of the cheerleaders? We should go off someplace where no one can hear us and practice until we've got it absolutely perfect."

"OK," Amy said. "I'll call everyone. Let's go way out to that field over there."

Robin had pointed out that the competition for a new cheer wasn't supposed to be until Wednesday, so Jessica had agreed not to compete if they would do her cheer today.

For the next ten minutes, all the cheerleaders practiced hard on Jessica's cheer. It took a little work to convince some of them to do the new cheer at all. Annie Whitman, Cara Walker, and Jeanie West seemed especially reluctant. But Jessica assured them they were being silly and there was no way it could possibly offend Claire. And besides, she reminded them, hadn't Claire said offensive things about cheerleaders?

That did the trick. By the time the scrimmage was ready to get underway, Jessica was more than satisfied. They had a cheer that was guaranteed to get Claire's attention off the game. And with any luck, that was all it would take to give Ken Matthews the upper hand in the competition.

Coach Schultz blew his whistle, signaling that the scrimmage was about to begin. Jessica felt her heart beating faster than normal. This wasn't just the most important intrasquad game Sweet Valley High had ever played. It was also her chance to humiliate Claire—in front of Danny Porter.

Terri was getting her clipboard ready when Claire came onto the field. She was wearing the regulation football uniform, complete with padding, and carrying her helmet in her arms. But despite a number of whistles and catcalls, she acted perfectly calm, as if nothing, or no one, could ruffle her composure. Terri tried to suppress her jealousy as she watched the other girl.

Coach Schultz explained that the team would be divided in two. Claire would be quarterback for the A team and Ken for the B team. All eyes would be on the two quarterbacks. Both assistant coaches were on hand to help Coach Schultz judge each quarterback's performance. The stands were packed with people: parents and friends of the players, classmates, and a number of people drawn by the publicity surrounding Claire.

The A team kicked off, and the scrimmage was underway. Tim caught the ball on the twenty-yard line and ran for ten yards. On the next play Ken faked a handoff, then ran like lightning up the middle of the field, dodging tackles as he ran.

"Go, Ken! Come on!" the fans in the bleachers started screaming.

Despite how upset she was, Terri couldn't help being drawn into the action. Ken was doing great.

Ken ran for forty yards before he was tackled at the thirty-yard line. The crowd went wild. Terri felt her breath quicken as she watched him.

But the B team didn't keep the ball for long.

The B team running back, Dave Pollock, fumbled on the next play, and the A team offense, led by Claire, lined up on the field.

On the A team's first possession, Claire faded back and threw a beautiful spiral that was easily caught by Danny Porter thirty yards upfield.

Now the crowd really went crazy. "Yeah, Claire! Show the guys how to play ball!" Terri heard Dana Larson holler.

Terri couldn't believe it. Was Claire going to outplay Ken?

Jessica jumped to her feet at the sideline and waved to the other cheerleaders. "Come on, guys. Don't you think it's time for our special cheer?"

Coach Schultz had called a time-out, and the players were standing at the sidelines. Claire had taken off her helmet and was wiping her face with a towel.

At Jessica's signal, the cheer began:

> "Who wants a guy
> when a girl like Claire
> can throw the ball
> from here to there?"

The audience hushed up to listen. A few people applauded when they heard the new cheer.

The cheerleaders had the full attention of both the crowd and the players. Jessica signaled again, and they launched into the next verse:

> "Who needs a guy
> when a girl gives more?
> She steals the ball,
> she makes the score!"

This brought more cheers from the stands. Claire was setting her water bottle down, a half-smile on her face, when Jessica signaled for the last and final verse of their "customized" cheer:

> "Who needs a guy
> when a girl instead
> can play like Claire?—
> We know about Ted!"

This last verse seemed to confuse the crowd, but there was a final spattering of applause. Jessica looked over to see Claire's reaction.

The effect of the cheer on Claire was absolutely astonishing. It was as if her blood had turned to ice. She stood frozen, her face white, her eyes wide and angry. There were two spots of color that rose in her cheeks. Trembling, she reached for her helmet, which she had set on the bench.

Coach Schultz was approaching her, but Claire didn't even appear to see him. Clutching her helmet in her hands, she started walking away from the bench—and off the field.

"Claire, where are you going?" Jessica heard the coach ask. "I'm in the middle of talking to you."

Claire turned, a frozen expression still on her face. "I'm leaving—I've had it," she said flatly.

"You can't leave! We're in the middle of a scrimmage!" Coach Schultz exclaimed.

"I don't care," Claire said, her voice perfectly emotionless. "I quit."

Coach Schulz looked completely baffled. But Claire didn't stick around for another minute. Looking straight ahead of her, she walked toward the locker room while the entire crowd gaped after her.

Jessica and the cheerleaders were as astonished as the rest of them.

"What did we say?" Robin gasped.

"Was it our cheer that made her leave?" Jeanie asked anxiously.

Jessica didn't know what to say. Even in her wildest dreams, she wouldn't have believed the cheer she'd written could actually drive Claire off the team!

Ten

Elizabeth Wakefield was shocked as she watched Claire walk off the field. How could they have made a cheer about Claire's dead brother? It was too awful!

"I don't believe what just happened," Todd said.

"Me, neither," Steven said, shaking his head.

"How could the cheerleaders have done something so cruel?" Elizabeth exclaimed. Now she understood why Jessica had been acting so mysteriously that morning. "Do you think they know who Ted was? I mean, how could they possibly have used his name like that—in a cheer? No wonder Claire is so upset!"

Coach Schultz blew furiously on his whistle, drawing their attention back to the field. "This scrimmage is going on. We're not here to make scenes, we're here to play ball. Dave Pollock, I want you to take over as quarterback for the A team. And I want you all to keep playing—*now*."

As the players got into position Steven turned to Elizabeth and said, "I don't know what's going on, but I think we'd better find out."

Elizabeth, Todd, and Steven scrambled down to the sidelines to confront Jessica and the others. Most of the cheerleaders looked guilty and confused, Elizabeth thought. Then she saw Jessica's triumphant expression, and she knew that somehow her twin was behind the cheer.

"Jess, would you mind explaining what you guys were trying to prove with that stunt?" Elizabeth demanded.

Jessica stared at her. "Private cheerleading stuff, Liz," she said airily. "Sorry, but I can't give away trade secrets."

"This isn't funny, Jessica," Elizabeth said angrily. "And at this point it isn't private, either!"

Jessica shrugged. "All we were trying to do was tease Claire a little bit. We were planning on doing something new with our cheers, anyway. Everyone's sick of the same old thing. We thought some customized cheers would be fun." She looked defensively at her twin. "Don't give me that look, Liz! You don't have to have a fit about it. We were only trying to spice things up a little. We didn't mean any harm."

117

"How can you say that?" Elizabeth sputtered. "I mean, what was that last line supposed to mean? Don't you know who Ted is? Were you deliberately trying to taunt Claire about her brother?"

"Brother?" Amy Sutton repeated. "We didn't think Ted was her *brother*. Terri said—"

Jessica cut her off. "Who says he's her brother? And so what if he is? I still don't understand why she was so upset about it."

Elizabeth couldn't believe her ears.

But the silence from the group in front of her told her the truth: They had no idea who Ted was. Someone else had fed them that line. Someone else was the real source of the cruelty here.

"Claire's older brother was a classmate of mine in college—Ted Middleton, who was diagnosed with cancer last year," Steven explained. "Before that, he was a big football hero with a brilliant career in front of him. Now—he's dead."

Jessica's hands flew to her face. "You mean . . . are you trying to tell us that we just did a cheer teasing Claire about her older brother— her *dead* older brother?" Her face went very pale.

"That's exactly what we're trying to tell you," Elizabeth said. "What were you guys trying to do to Claire? People have been taunting her all week. And now you guys go and mortify her in public, making her brother's death into a big joke."

Tears filled Jessica's eyes, and she looked at Elizabeth with genuine remorse. "We—honestly, Liz, we didn't know. We thought . . ."

"We just thought she had a crush on this guy Ted—that he was her boyfriend or something. We thought it would all be a big joke," Amy explained.

"Yeah," Cara agreed, looking sheepishly at Steven. "We were angry at Claire because she told Jess that she thought cheerleaders were ridiculous and that we should all be trying out for sports instead. We wanted to get back at her, but not like this."

"I don't understand how you could know about Ted and not know who he was," Elizabeth said, confused.

"We just assumed—" Jessica's voice broke off, and her eyes narrowed. "Terri Adams is the one who got us into this mess. She's the one who told us about Ted."

Elizabeth was sure her sister was mistaken. "You've got to be kidding. Terri Adams would never intentionally hurt someone's feelings."

"Well, Terri's the one who told us," Amy said, coming to Jessica's defense. "If anyone was trying to get to Claire, it was Terri. *She's* the one who deserves the blame for what just happened."

Elizabeth didn't know what to think or say. If Claire really *had* said something cruel about cheerleading, she didn't blame Jessica and the others for being annoyed. Maybe that didn't excuse their behavior, but if they didn't know who Ted was, they couldn't have guessed how much their cheer would hurt Claire.

But did Terri know? And if so, why would she want to play such a terrible trick on Claire?

Elizabeth waited until the scrimmage was over to talk to Terri.

"Listen, Terri, can I talk to you? Alone?" Elizabeth asked.

Terri looked up. "Uh . . . sure, Liz. What is it?"

Elizabeth sat down on the bleachers and motioned for Terri to sit beside her. "Listen, I'm probably running the risk of stepping into something that isn't any of my business, but I feel like I know you well enough to ask you about what happened here today." Terri gave her an uncertain look, but when she didn't say anything, Elizabeth went on. "Jessica and the other cheerleaders said you were the one who told them to put that taunting line about Claire's brother in their cheer."

"Claire's *brother*?" she repeated, looking confused. "What do you mean?"

Elizabeth blinked. Terri's confusion sounded genuine. Was it possible *she* didn't know who Ted was, either? "You must know about Ted. You're the one who told them to use his name to tease Claire, aren't you?"

"I was—I mean, I did," Terri said unhappily. "I know it was a stupid idea, but believe me, I didn't think it would upset her *that* much! I thought Ted was her old boyfriend or something . . . that she was a little shy about him; that it would be kind of funny to embarrass her in public." Terri blushed and fidgeted uncomfortably with her clipboard. "I know it was dumb, but it seemed like a good idea at the time."

Elizabeth took a deep breath. "And would it still seem like a good idea to you if you knew that not only was Ted Claire's older brother, but that he died of a brain tumor?"

Terri gasped and a look of horror crossed her face. "Oh, n-no!" she exclaimed.

"My brother was in college with Claire's brother. He was a big football hero till he got sick," Elizabeth said quietly.

Terri clapped her hand over her mouth. "I don't believe it," she whispered. "How could I have done that to her?"

"I don't get it, Terri," Elizabeth said. "Why on earth would you have wanted to embarrass Claire in the first place? What did she ever do to you, anyway?"

Terri looked despondently at Elizabeth without speaking. Then she began to cry.

"Look, it's a long, messy story," she choked out as tears streamed down her face. "I'm not going to be able to explain much of it. I've got to go apologize to her. I may have wanted to embarrass her, but I'd never have hurt her on purpose. Not like that."

"But what did you have against her?" Elizabeth asked again. "Why embarrass her at all?"

Terri wiped her eyes with the back of her sleeve. "I was jealous of her," she told Elizabeth. "Claire has everything. She's determined, she's confident . . . she's a fighter. And she's so pretty! Maybe you can't understand this, Liz, because you have everything, too. But I guess I just convinced myself that now that Ken's back to being the school hero again, he wouldn't want me anymore. He'd want someone like . . . Claire."

Elizabeth sounded very sad. "So you decided to get back at Claire instead of telling Ken what you were afraid of?"

Terri wiped at another tear. "I know I've been a total jerk. But, Liz, if I'd known who Ted was, if I'd had the slightest idea about his . . . dying, I never would have told Jessica and Amy to write a cheer about him! You have to believe me. It was just a mistake—a stupid, stupid mistake."

Elizabeth got to her feet. "I don't how much good it's going to do, but I have a suggestion."

"What?" Terri asked.

"I think we should go over to Claire's house right away. Maybe she hasn't blown it yet. Maybe it isn't too late for her to play on the team." Elizabeth's voice was determined. "But if she's going to act, she's going to have to do it now. Are you willing to tell Claire everything you just told me?"

Terri took a deep breath. "Yes," she said simply. "Even if she doesn't come back and play again, I owe her an apology. I want her to know how horrible I feel about what I've done."

Elizabeth nodded. "Then let's go," she said.

"Wait a minute," Terri said, grabbing Elizabeth's arm. When Elizabeth turned to look at her, Terri said, "Maybe I should go alone. After all, I'm the one who's responsible for this mess."

Elizabeth nodded, and on impulse, she gave Terri a hug. She could feel Terri trembling, and she knew how hard it was going to be for her to do this. Terri might not know it, Elizabeth thought, but she had real courage, too, just like Claire.

Claire opened the door after the second ring. She looked different to Terri. Her face was pale, and there were shadows under her eyes. She looked sad and vulnerable, Terri thought guiltily, hardly the formidable opponent she was expecting.

Terri took a deep breath and said, "Hi, Claire. Can I come in?"

Claire looked at her for a minute. "Well . . ." she said uncertainly. "I guess so."

Terri followed Claire into the Middletons' family room. The house was simple and spare, decorated in light pastel colors. Claire sat down on the couch, tucking her right foot under her leg. A cup of tea was steaming beside her, but she didn't touch it.

"Claire, listen. About what happened today," Terri began. "I owe you an enormous apology. You're not going to believe this, but that stuff about Ted—well, first off, it came from me, not the cheerleaders. I told them to use Ted's name."

Tears came to Claire's eyes, but she brushed them away quickly. "Why?" she asked.

"I thought . . . I didn't know who he was. I saw his picture that day in your locker, and I thought he might be an old boyfriend." She glanced down, feeling completely ashamed of herself.

Her confession seemed to strike a chord in Claire, who had been looking straight at Terri when she spoke. "It's weird. My parents were the ones who wanted to move after Teddy died.

124

They thought we needed a new house, a new neighborhood, a new school. I didn't agree with them. I guess I just wanted to stay there and fight it out. But once we moved here, it was such a big relief not to have to live with so much open mourning all the time. It was a relief to escape from how terrible we all felt when we lost him." She sighed. "But I was fooling myself. I don't know how I ever thought I could get over losing him."

"Claire—"

"I wasn't trying to hide anything," Claire went on, frowning. "I kept his picture in my locker because I was so proud of Ted. He's the one who taught me how to play football. He taught me a lot—about pride and standing up for myself. But I feel too strongly about his memory to talk about him with just anybody. Today, hearing his name used that way, to ridicule me . . ."

"I'm so sorry, Claire," Terri said. "I shouldn't have told the cheerleaders to use his name. And I never would have if I hadn't been so jealous of you."

"Jealous?" Claire looked completely surprised. "Why would *you* be jealous of *me*?"

"Oh, it was just everything! The way Ken talked about you. The way you two looked so happy playing ball together. Just everything."

Claire shook her head. "But Ken's crazy about

you, Terri. He talks about you all the time. He told me just yesterday that he never would have made it this far if it hadn't been for you."

Terri hung her head, feeling worse and worse. "I blew it," she whispered at last. "I know that. Look, Claire, I'm the one who deserves to be punished by all this stuff, not you. Won't you please go back to school and talk to Coach Schultz? Maybe he'll let you finish trying out."

"No way," Claire said firmly. "Look, I've learned a lot today, Terri. I'm sorry for the way it happened, but I was deluding myself. I could never play ball the way Ted did. What I did today, quitting like that, proves I don't have what it takes." She shook her head. "Forget it, Terri. I'm quitting football for good."

"Well, it's your decision," Terri said quietly, "but I think you're wrong. You've been an amazing role model to a lot of people. It might be easier to quit now than to go back and ask for a second chance, but if I'm hearing you right, that's not what your brother would have told you to do. He would've told you to keep playing."

Claire stared at her, and Terri saw that there were tears in her eyes.

"Go talk to the coach," Terri continued. "I've seen you play, Claire. You've got incredible talent. You ought to keep it up. Not because you owe it to your brother's memory, but because you owe it to yourself."

"Oh, Terri!" Claire said, wiping her eyes. "I've been missing him so much! But I guess you're right. I tell you what," she added. "I'll think about it," she said abruptly, "on one condition."

"What is that?" Terri asked.

"That you cut out this paranoia about Ken. Talk to him about this. If you keep doubting him, you'll probably screw things up." Claire pushed her hair back from her face. "I don't know the whole history between you two. But Ken's talked about you enough for me to know he loves you. Isn't *that* worth keeping?"

Terri swallowed hard. "I'll talk to Ken," she said slowly. "Does that mean you'll talk to the coach?"

Claire nodded. "Truce?" she asked, holding out her hand.

"Truce," Terri said.

Eleven

Terri took a deep breath. Going over to Claire's house had been hard—very hard—but what she was about to do seemed even harder.

She had driven straight over from Claire's house, and now she was standing out on the Matthewses' porch, trying to get up the nerve to ring the doorbell. She looked back at her mother's blue Volvo parked in the driveway. She could still leave, Terri thought to herself. She could just get right back in the car, drive off, and forget all about trying to make up.

But she'd made a deal with Claire. She had to go through with this. Terri leaned forward and pressed the bell.

"Terri, what a nice surprise," Mrs. Matthews said warmly when she opened the door. "Come in. Ken's upstairs resting. I think that scrimmage wore him out. Let me just tell him you're here."

Terri smiled and tried to ignore the nervous fluttering in her stomach. She waited for Ken in the family room, which was cheerful and comfortable, decorated in warm tones. Framed family photos covered the top of every surface, and Ken was in most of them. Terri picked up the photo closest to her. It was of Ken in his Gladiators' uniform, holding up the trophy he'd won last year—Most Valuable Player. A lump formed in her throat as she stared at the picture. She hadn't been very understanding since he decided to try out for quarterback. She knew her resistance came from love. She was afraid for him, afraid that the pressure would be too much, that he'd hurt himself. Still, she was his girlfriend. She should have been more enthusiastic when he decided to try out.

Terri looked up nervously when Ken entered the room. "Hi," he said in a low voice. "I didn't really expect to see you here. Not after what happened this morning. After what I said . . ."

Terri put her hand up to silence him. "Don't, Ken. Not until you hear what I have to say. Because, believe me, you're not going to like it."

Right then she felt that it would be easier to submit to any torture rather than tell Ken about her role in that day's fiasco. But she knew she had to tell him the truth. She wouldn't be comfortable around him until she did. Besides, it was time to clear the air between them.

As quickly as she could, she explained what had happened.

Ken couldn't believe his ears. "You did *what*?" he demanded.

"I know it's horrible. But the unbelievable part of it is, I didn't even know what I was doing. See, Jessica and the other cheerleaders wanted to make up a kind-of-mean, kind-of-funny cheer about Claire."

"Why?" Ken cut in. "Why her? Why not me? We're both trying out."

"Oh, Ken." Terri sighed. "You're not the kind of person anyone would ever want to pick on. And Claire . . . Well, listen to me, Ken. I know how much you admire her, but the truth is, she hasn't been that friendly to a lot of people since she moved here. She's made some real enemies. I think that's going to change now, because I don't think Claire's going to be so standoffish anymore. In fact, she told me today that she's going to apologize to the cheerleaders for something she said that made them furious. The point is, she *did* anger some people."

Ken looked convinced. "OK. So let's assume, for the moment, that Claire's kind of aloof," he said. "Maybe she even said something to upset the cheerleaders, and Jessica and Amy decided they wanted to get back at her by writing that cheer. Why did *you* get involved? And why did you feed them that line about Ted, even if you didn't know who he was? *Especially* if you didn't know who he was."

Terri reddened. This was going to be the hard part. "Ken, promise you won't have a fit if I tell you the truth."

Ken shook his head. "Terri, you and I have been through a lot. We trust each other. We tell each other things, remember?"

"Well, it hasn't been that way lately," Terri said. "But I guess it's time to start. The truth is, I was really jealous of Claire. I wanted to make her as miserable as I'd been feeling." She hung her head. "Dumb as it was, I thought going along with Jessica and Amy might make me feel better."

Ken looked incredulous. "You . . . jealous of Claire? Why?"

"Because—" Terri took a deep breath. "Because of you, Ken. Look, this may seem strange to you, but it hasn't been that easy for me accepting the fact that the old Ken Matthews is back. Remember, you and I never dated—not even once—before your accident. And I was afraid—" She broke off, unable to finish her sentence.

"You were afraid that now that I can see

131

again, I wouldn't want you for my girlfriend anymore," Ken finished for her.

Terri nodded, and Ken shook his head in disbelief. "Believe it or not, I thought about that a couple of times, too. I even wondered if maybe we should talk about it. I got the sense you were reluctant for me to try out for the team, and that got me a little mad. But then you were so great about it, the way you always are, so I just assumed . . . well, that you knew where you stood," Ken said.

Terri felt tears filling her eyes. "It's just that I care so much about you, Ken. The thought of losing you . . ."

Ken put his arms around Terri and held her close. "There's no way you could ever lose me," Ken said gruffly. "I'm not about to let that happen." He leaned over to brush a tear from her cheek, and his touch felt warm and tender. "But you still haven't told me why you were jealous of Claire."

Terri drew a deep, shaky breath. "Try to see it from my point of view. I was worried about you. I thought there was too much pressure on you to be the old Ken Matthews. But when I tried to talk to you about it, I guess I ended up seeming overprotective. Then along comes this wonderful quarterback who happens to be a great-looking girl. And I'm stuck on the sidelines, day after day, watching you two being paired up. 'Ken and Claire,' 'Claire and Ken.' That's what everyone's talking about." Terri straightened up unhappily. "I knew Claire wouldn't ever react the way I was. She wouldn't be protective—or paranoid. I couldn't help feeling these little pangs. And then you and I weren't getting along the way we usually do."

"And I guess I didn't help much, either. I know you've been a little worried about me—about my eyes, I mean. I guess I overreacted a little, too. I didn't want anything to get in the way of my chance to get back on the team. But as for my feelings about Claire, sure, I admire her. She's a brave girl and a good athlete, but that doesn't mean I *like* her—certainly not as anything but a friend. Terri, don't you know yet how I feel about you?"

Ken tipped Terri's face up so he was looking directly into her eyes. "It's because of you that I'm back out there on that field," he went on. "You're my best friend in the whole world, Terri. And you're more than that. You're the girl I'm in love with. Nothing's going to change that."

The note of determination in his voice made Terri shiver. "Ken, I love you, too." she whispered, tightening her arms around him.

After a long moment, Ken stepped back and looked at her, a frown on his face. "But where does all of this leave Claire?"

"She's going to talk to the coach," Terri told him, "and ask him if he'll still consider her for the team."

Ken nodded slowly. "That makes sense. I hope he agrees." He was quiet for a minute before adding, "It's eerie. I feel so sad when I think about Ted. I knew his name, but I never made the connection to Claire until today. After my accident, I didn't think I'd ever throw a pass again. It was like part of me had died. Being out there today, hearing that applause—" He looked urgently into Terri's eyes. "It felt so good, Terri. Can you understand how important it is for me to get back out there and try, even if I never get all the way back to where I was?"

"I do now," Terri said softly.

The kiss he gave her said more than any words could about how much she meant to him. And Terri knew then that everything was going to be all right between them.

Elizabeth and Terri were having lunch together on Monday when Claire came over. Her dark hair was tied back in a neat ponytail, and there was a tense look on her face.

"Hi," she said, sitting down next to Terri.

"Claire! I've been trying to find you all day,"

Terri exclaimed. "Did you find the coach? What did he say?"

"I just came back from talking to him." Claire shook her head. "I really feel like I've been put through the wringer."

"Tell us what he said," Elizabeth urged.

"Well, he wasn't exactly thrilled to see me. Before I could even open my mouth to apologize for what happened, he gave me a speech about not being a quitter. I don't want to bore you guys with the details, but basically he said that first of all, I should never have walked off the field, no matter what. Second, he said I was in an unusual situation because everyone was watching me. According to Coach Schultz, people—sexist people, that is—like to say girls are too emotional to play sports seriously. Too high-strung. He said I played right into people's expectations."

"That's kind of harsh, under the circumstances," Terri objected.

"Yeah, well, he did get human for just a second," Claire said, smiling. "He said that he knew my brother and really admired him, and that if he'd been in my shoes, he might have done the same thing."

All three girls were quiet for a minute.

"Wow," Terri finally said. "But what did he say about you playing for the Gladiators?"

"Well, he thinks Ken should be the first-string

quarterback," Claire said. "But he told me I could suit up for Saturday's game against Big Mesa. I guess I'll be the unofficial second-string quarterback. So at least I'll be part of the team."

"Yeah!" Terri cried.

"Claire, that's wonderful!" Elizabeth said.

"I'm pretty psyched," Claire said with a grin. She looked questioningly at Terri. "So what about you? Did you keep up your side of the bargain?"

Elizabeth turned to Terri and raised an eyebrow. "Bargain? What are you talking about?"

"It's a long story," Terri said. Then, turning to Claire, she added, "Let's just say everything's back on track, and, boy, is that a big relief."

Claire's green eyes brightened, and she gave Terri a high-five. "Way to go. Listen, I'd love to have lunch with you two, but I want to find Jessica and Amy and the rest of the cheerleaders. I said something pretty stupid after the Pumas game last week, and I want to apologize to them."

"Maybe we can have lunch tomorrow," Terri suggested.

"You're on." Claire looked down at Terri's lunch tray with a smile. "I'd better plan on eating a lot this week. If the coach is going to let me suit up for the game, I want to be ready to play. So you can count on it, Terri. Same time, same place—tomorrow."

Terri grinned as she watched Claire head for the cafeteria door. "You know, Liz," she said, "the Gladiators are lucky. They've gotten two really great quarterbacks out of these tryouts."

"Yeah," Elizabeth agreed. "And you're lucky, too. One of them is your boyfriend. And it looks like the other one is going to become a good friend!"

Twelve

Elizabeth and Enid crowded into the bleachers next to Todd just before the opening ceremonies at the Sweet Valley High–Big Mesa game. Todd had saved them places, but the stands were so packed, there wasn't much room.

"You guys almost missed the kickoff," Dana Larson scolded from where she sat just below them.

Elizabeth glanced at Enid. She wasn't going to say anything to the others, but the reason they were late was because Enid had been in tears when Elizabeth stopped by to pick her up. Apparently she and Hugh had decided to split up for a while, and while Enid thought it was the best thing, she was still pretty upset about it.

"Well, we're here now," Elizabeth said lightly,

trying to cover up for Enid so no one would ask her about Hugh.

As she spoke, Big Mesa's cheerleaders ran out onto the field, hurling their pom-poms in the air. Then Sweet Valley's cheerleaders rushed out to meet them. Opening ceremonies were under way, and the big game of the season was about to begin!

"How was Ken feeling this morning?" Enid asked Winston.

"Pretty good. He's really psyched," Winston said. "Apparently Coach Schultz had the whole team watch films of Big Mesa in action. They have a few really ace players—Peter Straus, for one, and then there's the star tackle, Matt Ambers. But Ken said the coach got them so fired up, they're really sure they can do it."

"Straus may be headed for a great college team," Todd said, "but my bet is that Ken will be able to nail Big Mesa down before the half."

Elizabeth scanned the area where the Gladiators were warming up. She saw Claire right away, in her uniform, stretching out on the grass next to Zack Johnson. And there was Terri, at the coach's table, her red Gladiators' cap swiveled backward, her face bright with happiness.

Terri took a deep breath. This was it—the game they'd all been waiting for.

She ran over to Ken to give him a hug before the action began. "How're you doing?" she asked him under her breath.

"OK. My eyes were bugging me a little bit this morning," he said in a low voice, "but I think once we get started—"

"You think you're OK to play?" Terri asked, concerned.

"Yeah, I think so. I've got to be," he said. He gave her a nervous smile. "Cross your fingers for me, Ter."

Terri didn't have a chance to say another word. Coach Schultz blew the whistle, and the whole team formed a huddle, crouching forward around him.

"Big Mesa's ready for us, I can tell," the coach was saying. "Defense, I want you all over Peter Straus. Remember those films we watched. You know how he moves, and you know how to stop him. Wherever he is, you are. And offense . . . I want you behind Ken. Listen up when he calls plays. He's in charge out there, and don't forget it. Now, tell me what you all need to do."

"Score!" everyone cried, slapping one another on the hands or shoulders.

Zack and Tad slapped Ken on the back, and Terri saw Claire jog up to shake his hand. "You can do it, Matthews," she cried. "Good luck."

Then all the players' voices were lost to Terri

as the announcer called out Big Mesa's starting lineup. Peter Straus jogged confidently out when his name was called. He was a big guy—bigger than Ken—and Terri had to admit he looked impressive.

Once all the Big Mesa players were out on the field, Sweet Valley's starting lineup was introduced by name and number. Then it was time for the kickoff, and the game was underway.

Terri could barely sit still. Every time Ken lunged for the ball, she felt herself lunging with him. When he raced up to Big Mesa's thirty-yard line, she felt her heart pound, as if it were she who was struggling through the intimidating line of defensive players.

Big Mesa was good—very good—but the Gladiators were playing better than they had ever played before. Their defense was strong, and in the first quarter Ken scored a touchdown, followed by the extra point from Danny Porter. Sweet Valley High was ahead, 7–0!

The cheerleaders went crazy.

"Second and ten!
That's our Ken!
See him score?
There will be more!"

Wild applause greeted Ken as he ran back to

the bench for a gulp of water before the second quarter began.

When the game resumed, Terri leaned forward anxiously on her seat. The second quarter wasn't off to as good a start as the first. Sweet Valley's defense began to falter, and they just weren't strong enough to hold Big Mesa back. They kept missing tackles, and from what Terri could see, Peter Straus was completing passes on every play. Eight minutes into the second quarter Big Mesa had evened the score at 7–7. For the rest of the quarter the two teams struggled to pull ahead, but neither side managed to score again.

Coach Schultz pulled the whole team aside for a pep talk during halftime. "We're holding 'em, you guys, but we've got to push for more. You all know what Big Mesa is like in the second half. Defense, you're looking sloppy out there. And offense, you're going to have to work harder. I want all of you to toughen up. This game means too much for us to let it slide through our fingers."

When Terri looked at Ken, she was surprised at how pale he looked. He was perspiring more than he ought to be, too, and once or twice she saw him pass his hand in front of his eyes.

"Are you all right?" she asked him when the coach had finished and went over to talk to the assistant coaches. "You don't look so great."

"I'm fine," he muttered, not looking at her.

Terri didn't know what to do. She didn't want to be overprotective again, but she was really worried. Before she could say anything else, however, Coach Schultz came over to discuss a play with Ken. That was that, Terri thought, watching anxiously as the coach led Ken off. She had lost her chance to talk to him.

Before she knew it, the third quarter was starting, and Terri went over to stand near the bench. Claire was sitting next to two juniors on the Gladiators' team, Greg Herly and Don Cavendish. Neither had been very receptive to Claire during the tryouts for quarterback, but today, in the excitement of the game, they were talking to her as they would any other teammate. So was Tim Nelson, who was out after the half with a sore ankle.

Tim turned to Claire, and Terri heard him say, "What's with Ken? He's acting weird out there. Watch him. His last two passes were way off."

It was true. Terri had already noticed, and so had Big Mesa's defense. On the next play Ken backed up, but he seemed to falter before he threw. The pass was way off and was easily intercepted by a Big Mesa player. In the next instant that player was streaking upfield for another touchdown. With the extra point, the score was now 14 to 7.

The mood on the bench was nervous. Everyone crowded around, jumping up and down for a better view. The Gladiators couldn't seem to make a comeback. At the start of the fourth quarter the score was still stuck at 14–7.

That was when disaster struck. Ken backed up to throw. He paused for a split second, stumbled, and shook his head a little, as if to clear it. Terri felt her heart leap into her throat. It was his eyes, she knew it. Ken couldn't see.

In a moment of panic, Ken lofted the ball far from any Sweet Valley receiver. Big Mesa's Troy Isaacs dove for it, and soon a pile of players was on top of him. But when they got up, Troy was still gripping the ball to his chest.

Big Mesa had intercepted the ball again!

As the Gladiators walked unhappily to the sidelines, Terri rushed over to see if Ken was all right. He'd taken off his helmet and was wiping his eyes with the back of his hand.

"I don't know what's going on out there. I can't see," he muttered.

"Are you all right, son?" Coach Schultz asked him.

Ken shook his head. "I'm blowing it for the team. I think you should take me out, Coach."

Three plays later Big Mesa had to punt the ball, and Coach Schultz made his decision. "Matthews, you're on the bench. Middleton, you're in."

144

Claire got to her feet, staring at the coach. "Wh-what?" she stammered.

"I said you're in," the coach repeated. "Go on."

Ken slapped her on the back. "Go get 'em, Claire," he said.

Claire took a deep breath and ran out onto the field. The whole team started chanting, "Claire! Claire! Claire! Claire!"

Terri put her arm around Ken. "Do you feel all right?"

Ken nodded. "I'm fine. I guess I just wasn't ready to play yet," he said, wiping off his face. "My eyes just blacked out. I couldn't see a thing. It was just for a second, but that was enough to really screw things up." Ken shook his head and looked out at the field. "I hope Claire can pull this off. I haven't done her much of a favor, leaving us this far behind," he mumbled.

Sweet Valley's offense squared off against Big Mesa's powerful defense. Claire crouched down, leading the group in a huddle. "Thirty-one wedge," she cried. "I'll carry the ball."

The offensive line opened up on either side of her, leaving a gaping hole in the middle. Claire bolted through center field. She ran even faster than Terri had seen in practice, as if adrenaline and passion carried her forward. Within seconds she was gliding over the chalk line in the end zone, home free. Claire Middleton had scored a touchdown!

The crowd went crazy. All of Sweet Valley's fans rose to their feet in one enormous wave, giving their new quarterback a standing ovation. Terri felt her heart begin to pound. For the first time she had a sense that they could do it. There were only four minutes left in the game, but they could still win. She could feel Ken straining beside her, and she knew that every part of him was out there on the field with Claire, fighting to win.

Terri had never seen a game as tense and as thrilling as this one. Sweet Valley's offense played like pros, and through it all, Claire was there, calling plays, throwing perfect passes, and running with speed and agility that seemed to dazzle and confound Big Mesa. Then, with less than a minute to play, Claire threw a perfect pass for the final touchdown. With the extra point conversion, Sweet Valley was ahead 21–14. They'd done it! Seconds later the buzzer sounded, and the crowd went crazy.

Claire Middleton had won the game for them!

Terri watched as Ken leapt to his feet and ran onto the field to congratulate Claire.

"You were awesome!" he cried, giving her a big hug.

"Tell me what happened. Are you OK? Are your eyes all right?" Claire asked.

"I'm fine, Claire. I just had no business playing today. The doctor told me I might have blackouts or blurred vision for another couple of months. It was just . . . well, I wanted to play so badly. I took a risk, and I shouldn't have. I'm just glad you were around to save the day."

Claire shook her head. "You had every business playing, Ken. You were doing a great job," she said.

Coach Schultz was on his way over, a big smile on his face. But before he reached her, the entire football team rushed over to her. Lifting Claire easily up on their shoulders, they began cheering.

Terri watched her with admiration. She couldn't get over Claire Middleton. It was incredible seeing her victory. And one of the best moments came when Jessica ran out into the field, leading the cheerleaders in a brand-new cheer for Claire.

"Who needs a guy when you've got Claire?
She runs, she scores, she gets you there!
Of all the heroes, she's the best!
The greatest player in the west!"

With a resounding chorus of "Yeah, Claire!" the cheerleaders followed behind the team as they carried Claire around the field. There was no doubt about it: Claire was the hero of the day. And watching her, Terri felt nothing but joy and pride for her new friend.

"What an incredible game," Jessica said to Amy Sutton as they took off their cheerleading outfits in the locker room. "Claire's really changed my mind about girls playing football!"

"Yours isn't the only mind she's changed," Amy said with a giggle. "You should've seen the shocked expressions on Peter Straus's and Matt Ambers's faces when the *News* came to do the after-game interview. Having to stand side by side with a *girl*—and one who'd beaten them, no less." She grinned. "I never thought I'd be saying this, but I'm proud of Claire."

"Me, too," Jessica said as she shimmied into her jeans.

They had done some other new cheers besides the revised one for Claire at that day's game, and Jessica had been pleased with the crowd's reception of them. Cara Walker had won the competition with her cheer for Ken, but Jessica didn't even care. She'd still gotten to do her new cheer for Claire, and that was the one that had gotten the most attention.

"She ought to try out for that spot on Eric Parker's television show," Amy continued.

Jessica raised her eyebrows. "What spot?" she asked.

"Oh, that's right—I guess you don't know about it yet," Amy said airily. "Sometimes I forget that I hear about these things first, being the daughter of a TV personality and all." Amy's mother was a local sportscaster.

"What are you talking about?" Jessica demanded.

"Eric Parker's looking for a high school student to be on his show. Someone who typifies the all-American student. But now that I think about it, I guess Claire is really too unusual. He wants someone a little more rounded, not a superjock or anything." Amy combed out her hair and added, "I happened to mention the show to Lila yesterday, and Lila seems to think she's exactly what Eric Parker is looking for."

The wheels in Jessica's mind began to whirl. Imagine getting the chance to be on a TV talk show. The whole country would be watching her! "Lila isn't typical," Jessica said dismissively. "For one thing, her father owns half of Southern California. How typical is that?"

Amy shrugged. "Why are you so upset, Jess? You're not interested in trying out yourself, are you?"

"I just might be," Jessica retorted.

Jessica was happy for Claire, but in her opinion the new quarterback had received enough attention. It was high time Jessica Wakefield got back into the limelight, where she belonged! She wouldn't mind her own share of attention. And if Lila Fowler thought she was going to get the spot on Eric Parker's talk show, she would find out that Jessica wasn't about to let friendship get in the way of stardom!

Will Jessica get her big chance to be on TV? Find out in Sweet Valley High #71, **STARRING JESSICA!**

SWEET VALLEY HIGH

COULD *YOU* BE THE NEXT SWEET VALLEY READER OF THE MONTH?

ENTER BANTAM BOOKS' SWEET VALLEY CONTEST & SWEEPSTAKES IN ONE!

Calling all Sweet Valley Fans! Here's a chance to appear in a Sweet Valley book!

We know how important Sweet Valley is to you. That's why we've come up with a Sweet Valley celebration offering exciting opportunities to have YOUR thoughts printed in a Sweet Valley book!

"How do I become a Sweet Valley Reader of the Month?"

It's easy. Just write a one-page essay (no more than 150 words, please) telling us a little about yourself, and why you like to read Sweet Valley books. We will pick the best essays and print them along with the winner's photo in the back of upcoming Sweet Valley books. Every month there will be a new Sweet Valley High Reader of the Month!

And, there's more!

Just sending in your essay makes you eligible for the Grand Prize drawing for a trip to Los Angeles, California! This once-in-a-life-time trip includes round-trip airfare, accommodations for 5 nights (economy double occupancy), a rental car, and meal allowances. (Approximate retail value: $4,500.)

Don't wait! Write your essay today.
No purchase necessary. See the next page for Official rules.

ENTER BANTAM BOOKS' SWEET VALLEY READER OF THE MONTH SWEEPSTAKES

OFFICIAL RULES:

READER OF THE MONTH ESSAY CONTEST

1. <u>No Purchase Is Necessary.</u> Enter by hand printing your name, address, date of birth and telephone number on a plain 3" x 5" card, and sending this card along with your essay telling us about yourself and why you like to read Sweet Valley books to:

READER OF THE MONTH
SWEET VALLEY HIGH
BANTAM BOOKS
YR MARKETING
666 FIFTH AVENUE
NEW YORK, NEW YORK 10103

2. <u>Reader of the Month Contest Winner.</u> For each month from June 1, 1990 through December 31, 1990, a Sweet Valley High Reader of the Month will be chosen from the entries received during that month. The winners will have their essay and photo published in the back of an upcoming Sweet Valley High title.

3. Enter as often as you wish, but each essay must be original and each entry must be mailed in a separate envelope bearing sufficient postage. All completed entries must be postmarked and received by Bantam no later than December 31, 1990, in order to be eligible for the Essay Contest and Sweepstakes. Entrants must be between the ages of 6 and 16 years old. Each essay must be no more than 150 words and must be typed double-spaced or neatly printed on one side of an 8 1/2" x 11" page which has the entrant's name, address, date of birth and telephone number at the top. The essays submitted will be judged each month by Bantam's Marketing Department on the basis of originality, creativity, thoughtfulness, and writing ability, and all of Bantam's decisions are final and binding. Essays become the property of Bantam Books and none will be returned. Bantam reserves the right to edit the winning essays for length and readability. Essay Contest winners will be notified by mail within 30 days of being chosen. In the event there are an insufficient number of essays received in any month which meet the minimum standards established by the judges, Bantam reserves the right not to choose a Reader of the Month. Winners have 30 days from the date of Bantam's notice in which to respond, or an alternate Reader of the Month winner will be chosen. Bantam is not responsible for incomplete or lost or misdirected entries.

4. Winners of the Essay Contest and their parents or legal guardians may be required to execute an Affidavit of Eligibility and Promotional Release supplied by Bantam. Entering the Reader of the Month Contest constitutes permission for use of the winner's name, address, likeness and contest submission for publicity and promotional purposes, with no additional compensation.

5. Employees of Bantam Books, Bantam Doubleday Dell Publishing Group, Inc., and their subsidiaries and affiliates, and their immediate family members are not eligible to enter the Essay Contest. The Essay Contest is open to residents of the U.S. and Canada (excluding the province of Quebec), and is void wherever prohibited or restricted by law. All applicable federal, state, and local regulations apply.

READER OF THE MONTH SWEEPSTAKES

6. Sweepstakes Entry. No purchase is necessary. Every entrant in the Sweet Valley High, Sweet Valley Twins and Sweet Valley Kids Essay Contest whose completed entry is received by December 31, 1990 will be entered in the Reader of the Month Sweepstakes. The Grand Prize winner will be selected in a random drawing from all completed entries received on or about February 1, 1991 and will be notified by mail. Bantam's decision is final and binding. Odds of winning are dependent on the number of entries received. The prize is non-transferable and no substitution is allowed. The Grand Prize winner must be accompanied on the trip by a parent or legal guardian. Taxes are the sole responsibility of the prize winner. Trip must be taken within one year of notification and is subject to availability. Travel arrangements will be made for the winner and, once made, no changes will be allowed.

7. 1 Grand Prize. A six day, five night trip for two to Los Angeles, California. Includes round-trip coach airfare, accommodations for 5 nights (economy double occupancy), a rental car -- economy model, and spending allowance for meals. (Approximate retail value: $4,500.)

8. The Grand Prize winner and their parent or legal guardian may be required to execute an Affidavit of Eligibility and Promotional Release supplied by Bantam. Entering the Reader of the Month Sweepstakes constitutes permission for use of the winner's name, address, and the likeness for publicity and promotional purposes, with no additional compensation.

9. Employees of Bantam Books, Bantam Doubleday Dell Publishing Group, Inc., and their subsidiaries and affiliates, and their immediate family members are not eligible to enter this Sweepstakes. The Sweepstakes is open to residents of the U.S. and Canada (excluding the province of Quebec), and is void wherever prohibited or restricted by law. If a Canadian resident, the Grand Prize winner will be required to correctly answer an arithmetical skill-testing question in order to receive the prize. All applicable federal, state, and local regulations apply. The Grand Prize will be awarded in the name of the minor's parent or guardian. Taxes, if any, are the winner's sole responsibility.

10. For the name of the Grand Prize winner and the names of the winners of the Sweet Valley High, Sweet Valley Twins and Sweet Valley Kids Essay Contests, send a stamped, self-addressed envelope entirely separate from your entry to: Bantam Books, Sweet Valley Reader of the Month Winners, Young Readers Marketing, 666 Fifth Avenue, New York, New York 10103. The winners list will be available after April 15, 1991.

☐	27650	**AGAINST THE ODDS #51**	$2.95
☐	27720	**WHITE LIES #52**	$2.95
☐	27771	**SECOND CHANCE #53**	$2.95
☐	27856	**TWO BOY WEEKEND #54**	$2.95
☐	27915	**PERFECT SHOT #55**	$2.95
☐	27970	**LOST AT SEA #56**	$2.95
☐	28079	**TEACHER CRUSH #57**	$2.95
☐	28156	**BROKEN HEARTS #58**	$2.95
☐	28193	**IN LOVE AGAIN #59**	$2.95
☐	28264	**THAT FATAL NIGHT #60**	$2.95
☐	28317	**BOY TROUBLE #61**	$2.95
☐	28352	**WHO'S WHO #62**	$2.95
☐	28385	**THE NEW ELIZABETH #63**	$2.95
☐	28487	**THE GHOST OF TRICIA MARTIN #64**	$2.95
☐	28518	**TROUBLE AT HOME #65**	$2.95
☐	28555	**WHO'S TO BLAME #66**	$2.95
☐	28611	**THE PARENT PLOT #67**	$2.95
☐	28618	**THE LOVE BET #68**	$2.95
☐	28636	**FRIEND AGAINST FRIEND #69**	$2.95
☐	28767	**MS. QUARTERBACK #70**	$2.95

Buy them at your local bookstore or use this page to order.

— — — — — — — — — — — — — — — —

Bantam Books, Dept. SVH7, 414 East Golf Road, Des Plaines, IL 60016

Please send me the items I have checked above. I am enclosing $_____
(please add $2.00 to cover postage and handling). Send check or money
order, no cash or C.O.D.s please.

Mr/Ms _____

Address _____

City/State _____ Zip _____

SVH7–11/90

Please allow four to six weeks for delivery.
Prices and availability subject to change without notice.

MURDER AND MYSTERY STRIKES

SWEET VALLEY HIGH®

America's favorite teen
series has a hot new line of
Super Thrillers!

It's super excitement, super suspense, and super thrills as Jessica
and Elizabeth Wakefield put on their detective caps in the new
SWEET VALLEY HIGH SUPER THRILLERS! Follow these
two sleuths as they witness a murder…find themselves running
from the mob…and uncover the dark secrets of a mysterious
woman. SWEET VALLEY HIGH SUPER THRILLERS are
guaranteed to keep you on the edge of your seat!

YOU'LL WANT TO READ THEM ALL!

☐ #1: DOUBLE JEOPARDY   26905-4/$2.95
☐ #2: ON THE RUN   27230-6/$2.95
☐ #3: NO PLACE TO HIDE   27554-2/$2.95
☐ #4: DEADLY SUMMER   28010-4/$2.95

HAVE YOU READ THE LATEST!
SWEET VALLEY STARS

☐ #1: LILA'S STORY   28296-4/$2.95
☐ #2: BRUCE'S STORY   28464-9/$2.95
☐ #3: ENID'S STORY   28576-9/$2.95

Bantam Books, Dept. SVH5, 414 East Golf Road, Des Plaines, IL 60016

Please send me the items I have checked above. I am enclosing $_____
(please add $2.00 to cover postage and handling). Send check or money
order, no cash or C.O.D.s please.

Mr/Ms _____

Address _____

City/State _____ Zip _____

SVH5-12/90

Please allow four to six weeks for delivery.
Prices and availability subject to change without notice.